MW00761729

Pink Angel

Hunter's Past

BEV MAGEE

authorHOUSE®

AuthorHouse™
1663 Liberty Drive
Bloomington, IN 47403
www.authorhouse.com
Phone: 1-800-839-8640

Published by AuthorHouse 3/2/2012

ISBN: 978-1-4685-5833-3 (e)
ISBN: 978-1-4685-5835-7 (hc)
ISBN: 978-1-4685-5834-0 (sc)

Library of Congress Control Number: 2012903840

Chapter 1

Hunter woke with a moan the next morning. He pushed himself up off his bed and swung his legs over the side. Cradling his head in his hands, he tried to dispel the images still invading his thoughts. They were the same images that kept him from sleeping last night. His head, throbbing from the lack of sleep, was keeping him from seeing straight.

Nitika had told him she loved him. They had spent glorious nights together. And now, a stranger shows up claiming to be her future husband. Maybe he was the reason that she didn't want to marry. Maybe what he and Nitika shared was only a fling that she would end when it was time to marry What's His Name.

Hunter heard the breakfast bell, but wasn't in the mood to eat. Slowly he dressed, still thinking about what happened yesterday. Never before had he felt like this. Not even when he was forced to leave Irena behind. The men would be waiting for him, so he forced himself to hurry. Lounging around the bunkhouse, the men watched their bedraggled foreman approach. Nitika came out of the main house as he joined the men.

He couldn't bear to look at her as she gave out orders for the day.

Slowly the men began to drift out to do their jobs for the day. Dyami was sitting on the front porch when Hunter finally saddled up and rode out. Nitika joined him once she watched Hunter leave.

"You need to talk to him."

"I'm not going to beg him to listen to me. When he's ready to talk, I'll be here."

"Yeah, but will he?"

Colton came out nursing a cup of coffee. "When's breakfast around here?"

"Breakfast is long over Colton. But Anna might be able to scratch something up for you. She's working on the noon meal now," Nitika said annoyed with the interruption.

"Is there really a need to get up this early? The sun's barely up."

"Son, we've already got three hours of work done before breakfast."

Colton brushed away a speck of dirt on his jacket. "Once we're married, we'll just hire a manager to handle such things. There's no reason to get up before the sun rises," he muttered heading for the cookhouse.

Doc noticed that Hunter had been sitting in the same position for the past ten minutes. Soon, the herd would be beyond him and the others might know he was sleeping in the saddle. The old surgeon went over and tapped Hunter on the shoulder with his rope. Hunter's head came up with a jerk, his hand dropping to his hip.

"You're supposed to do that at night in a bed." Hunter only stared at him. "I know what's eating you. You've got to go to her Son."

"And say what? She's the one who lied."

"Did you ever ask her?"

Hunter watched the cattle for a few moments. "No. I just assumed she was unattached."

"Well, she might still be, Hunter. She's mighty choosy about her men. I don't see her keeping a man like Colton Dragon." He continued once he saw Hunter wasn't going to talk. "You can't wait for her to come to you, because she won't. She's not about to beg a man

2

to do anything." Hunter grinned. "I don't even want to know what that's about, Son. Whatever is between the two of you is your own business."

Doc rode off, leaving Hunter with images of his nights with Nitika. She had seemed very surprised to see Colton ride into the yard. Maybe she was trying to hide from him. He definitely didn't seem like her kind of man. Colton was too dandified to want to live out here. Nitika wasn't about to leave the ranch after having to fight so hard to keep it.

Anna came stomping into the dining room at noon and dropped the dishes on the table. Dyami had to sidestep the elderly cook as she bustled around the room setting up for the few men who were working around the house. Those out in the pastures had taken their lunch with them. When one of the dishes missed the table and shattered on the floor, she began to scream.

"It's just a dish Anna," Dyami soothed. "We can have it replaced."

"It's not the dish Mr. Brodie," she said slumping in a nearby chair. "It's that man, Colton. What's he doing here anyway?"

"He claims he's here to marry Nitika."

"I don't believe that," she fumed. "I don't believe your daughter would be that stupid. Not with a man like Hunter Tilton living under her roof. That man is impossible."

"What did he do," Dyami asked now amused at the woman's tirade.

"He came down looking for something to eat. I gave him what I could, but it wasn't good enough. He wanted me to carry it up here and *serve* him. I told him I didn't have time and that he was just going to have to make due. Then he says that he was going to have me replaced as soon as possible with a more agreeable cook. I just wanted to take that little whelp over my knee and tan his backside." She stood up and pointed her finger at Dyami. "That boy better be out of here soon, or one of us will be carted out of here feet first."

3

"I'll see what I can do Anna. Just try not to break any more dishes over him, okay?"

Anna managed to wedge herself beside Nitika once lunch was served. Dyami was already seated on Nitika's right, forcing Colton to sit on the other side of him. The men were silent as they quickly ate their meal and hustle back out to finish their jobs. Nitika began to stack dishes on the sideboard when Colton grabbed her arm.

"Let the help do that, my Dear. We haven't had time to talk since I arrived."

"I'll help you Anna," Dyami quickly volunteered before the cook could open her mouth.

Colton led Nitika out onto the front porch. "Really, we need to hire more help around here. It doesn't look good for your father to be doing manual labor."

"He enjoys working, and so do I. There's a lot to be done around here."

"No wife of mine is going to get her hands dirty doing work. I'll make sure there's plenty of servants to wait on you hand and foot."

Nitika pulled free of his grasp. "You are certainly generous with my money."

"I'm just looking out for your best interests, Love. I only want the best for you."

Dandy rode over to the porch and overheard the last part of their conversation. What he heard left a bad taste in his mouth. It was clear to him that this citified dude was only after Nitika's money. He only hoped Nitika saw through his lies.

"We got the swamp fenced off, even though it don't need it."

"I have my reasons Dandy. I'm protecting more than just my animals from the muck."

"If you say so Ma'am. You seen Hunter lately?"

"I sent him after Doc and his group to round up Old Red Nose and his ladies."

"Why you bringing him closer to home anyhow Ma'am? He's just gonna take them back where they were."

"I'm hoping the better grass in the north pasture will convince him to stay there. He's stripping his valley of anything useful. I want good strong calves from him. There's not enough grass left in his valley for that."

Nitika watched Hunter push the food around on his plate at supper. The man was refusing to look at her. Perhaps she was going to have to break down and talk with him. But as hurt as he was, he might not be willing to listen to her. After the others had eaten and were gone, Hunter still sat there. Handing the last dish to Anna, she sat down across from him.

"We need to talk," Hunter said, finally looking at her.

"Let's go to my office."

Once there, Hunter began to pace. "Where did you and Colton meet?"

"Chicago about six months ago."

He nodded. "How long-. When did he propose?"

"About three weeks later."

Hunter took a deep breath. This was the one question he didn't want to hear the answer to. "So, how soon is the wedding?"

Chapter 2

Nitika motioned him to the couch. Hunter reluctantly sat down, fearing the worse. Why else would she be hesitating? She sat down next to him and took his hand. "There isn't going to be a wedding."

"What do you mean," he asked stunned.

"It means, I never accepted his proposal. He's asked me several times to marry him, but I turned him down every time. He's only after my money."

"How do you know that?"

"Because he didn't propose until after he found out that Father left me his half of the ranch in his will. Now, I can't get rid of him."

"Is that why you decided to move out here? To get away from him?"

"No," she said moving closer to him. "Uncle Alex asked me to come live with him. He said it was getting lonely for him out here. Little did I know, he planned on us meeting."

"So what do we do about Lover Boy, then?"

Nitika heard the door rattle before Colton entered her office. He spotted the two of them sitting close together. Colton frowned when he saw Nitika holding Hunter's hand. She could see that he wanted to get between them, but didn't dare try in her office.

"I was hoping we'd be able to have some time alone. There's a lot of planning to do before the wedding. And I'd like to get started."

"You're wasting your time Colton. I don't ever plan on marrying you. I never have, nor will I ever love you. Go find yourself another rich woman to prey on. I'm sure there's plenty out there desperate enough to marry even you."

Colton clicked his tongue. "You can't seriously think that this *cowboy* can give you the life you deserve. You're better than that. No, I won't permit you to throw your life away on a no-account like him."

Nitika felt the muscles in Hunter's arm tense at the insult. She tightened her grip slightly. Hunter took the hint and settled back against the couch, though he never fully relaxed. Colton was trying to goad him into a fight and they both knew it. And Nitika didn't want to give Colton the satisfaction.

"The lady has a mind of her own. It's up to her to decide who she wants around. And it's quite clear that you have worn out your welcome here."

Colton scoffed. "She's a woman. She doesn't know what's good for her. That's why she needs a man like me around."

"Alright, that's enough," she shouted. "I want you packed up and gone by tomorrow, Colton. You are no longer a guest in my house. And if you won't leave, I have enough men here who can throw you off and keep you off."

Colton gave her a consoling smile. "You've just been through a terrible ordeal. You're not thinking straight. You don't know what you're saying. That's why I have to stay. You need someone around here who's rational."

With that said, Colton excused himself. He looked back to see if Hunter would follow him. Instead, the foreman sat motionless staring at him as he left the room. Once the door closed behind Colton, Nitika began to shake. Hunter thought to comfort her, but she jumped up before he could move.

"Just who does he think he is," she fumed, pacing the floor.

"Coming into *my* house and ordering *me* around. If I'd had my gun, we could have resolved this thing real quick."

"So what are you going to do now," Hunter asked humored by her outburst.

"I'm going to make sure he gets escorted off my land right after breakfast," she said plopping back down on the couch.

"Why not before," Hunter asked with a yawn.

"Because I don't want him telling everyone I threw a hungry man off my ranch."

"You're too soft hearted," he mumbled as he drew her closer.

"I'm not always-," she commented as she looked up at him.

But whatever else she would have said would remain to herself. The sleepless night had finally caught up with Hunter. He had snuggled her against him as he slept. Gently freeing herself, Nitika took Hunter's boots off. She went across the hall to the linen closet and brought back a blanket. Once Hunter was covered, she trimmed the lamp and closed the door. Nitika gasped when she turned around.

"Something I shouldn't know about Angel?"

"No. I mean, Hunter fell asleep in there and I didn't want to wake him Father."

"I would have thought that you'd want to join him."

"Not with Colton Dagon in this house I wouldn't. I don't trust him not to barge in on us."

Dyami chuckled. "That's my girl. I didn't think you liked the man. What are we doing about Mr. Dagon?"

"I told him to leave in the morning. Chances are, the men are going to have to help him to the border."

"Why's that," Dyami asked keeping pace with her.

"He says I need a man like him around after such a traumatic ordeal. He says I'm not thinking clearly."

"Dagon certainly doesn't know you, does he?"

"No, but he'd liked to get to know my money."

Colton strolled down the stairs at ten o'clock the next morning, a triumphant smile on his face. He half expected Nitika to send the hands up to his room and physically remove him from the house earlier. When that didn't happen, he knew she was bluffing. Women just weren't the forceful type. Now he had to find a way to get rid of the foreman.

That man was the only thing standing in his way. Without him around, Nitika would have no one else to lean on when she got in trouble. The way he was cozying up to Nitika, Colton knew the man was after her money too. Hunter wasn't even man enough to stand up for himself last night. That's what happens when you work for a woman, he thought as he entered the dining room, you forget how to be a man.

The room was abandoned, but there was a plate sitting on the sideboard on a hot plate. He lifted the napkin and saw what was left for him. Colton wrinkled his nose at the food. Steak and potatoes was not his idea of breakfast. The cook definitely has to go, he noted as he took the warm dish over to the table. Nitika came in as he was finishing up. Grinning, he leaned back in his chair.

"I see you found your breakfast," she stated, standing hip-shot in the doorway.

"It wasn't what I wanted, but it will do. Now, how about we start planning our wedding?"

Nitika planted her feet. "I told you last night to be packed. Are you?"

"Now Sweetheart, I know you didn't mean what you said last night. It was that foreman of yours that was telling you things. Can't you see he's trying to have you for himself?"

"Not anymore than I want him. I guess I can always send your things later. Right now the only thing I want is you off my land."

Doc came in with his thumbs hooked in his belt. "His horse is saddled and ready to go, is he?"

"He hasn't packed yet. I guess that means the boys are going to have to help him."

"I'll go get them right now," Doc said with a nod.

Nitika followed Doc outside with Colton right on her heels. It was obvious that she planned on carrying out her threat. He hoped

9

he could talk her out of this. His plans all depended on having Nitika as his wife. Colton couldn't let her ruin his new life.

"I see your foreman is poisoning your mind again. So, I will leave for now. But you have to give me at least an hour to pack," he insisted.

"You came here with one small bag two days ago. You don't have much to pack. In fact, why don't I show you how quickly you can pack."

Nitika headed back to the house, intending to throw his things out the window. Colton grabbed her arm and turned her around to face him. Immediately, she drew her gun and pointed it at him. She was not going to let him tell her what to do. No man did that to her.

"I want you off my land and out of my life before noon. After that, you will be considered an intruder. My men have orders to shoot any intruders on sight." Colton grinned and leaned into her gun. She cocked and shoved the pistol against his chest. "You won't be the first man I shot."

"Mind telling me what's going on," the sheriff asked.

Chapter 3

"Nothing I can't handle Sheriff. Mr. Dagon here was just leaving."

"Yeah," Donnish said shifting in his saddle. "I can see that. I'll be more than happy to escort him back to town. There's no telling what kind of trouble he might encounter along the way."

"What brings you out here Charlie," Dyami asked handing the man a cup of coffee.

"Just thought I'd let you know that your friends got the Oldriches shipped off to Texas. Your Ranger friend is escorting them all the way. Never would have believed that kid was a Ranger."

"Are you just going to sit there and let Miss Brodie point a gun at me, Sheriff," Colton screeched.

"What gun," he asked innocently. "If you're ready, I'd like to get back to town before dark."

Protesting, Colton mounted his horse and fell in line with the sheriff. Clearly he wasn't going to get any kind of help from the law. Whatever he did to rid himself of the meddling foreman, he was on his own. The trip to Santa Fe was a quiet one. The sheriff didn't go out of his way to be friendly.

"Hotel's over there," the sheriff said pointing to a frame building across the street from his office. "It's not too full right now. You should be able to get a room for the night. The train won't be here until the morning."

"Are you telling me to leave town, Sheriff?"

"Not at all," Donnish denied. "I just figured you might want to know when the train came through."

Colton watched the man's retreating back before going to the courthouse. Everyone in this town seemed to be protecting Nitika. One way or another, he planned to have her for his own. After all, he was a much better choice than that poverty-prone cowboy she seemed to like. While his wealth didn't compare to hers, it was greater than anything her foreman could offer.

The sheriff was watching when the train pulled into the station. He waved to Colton as he boarded the coach car. Donnish had some nerve treating him like a tramp. His biggest disappointment was the way Nitika treated him, especially after all the trouble he went through to find her.

He had known her uncle had a ranch somewhere in New Mexico and that she had inherited her father's half after his supposed death. But there was so much land around Santa Fe that belonged to one ranch or another, that it took him awhile to locate her ranch. It was when he stopped at one little shack that he found out that Alexander Brodie had been killed in a stampede.

After looking at the deed in the courthouse, he knew that Nitika now owned the entire ranch. That meant that once he convinced her to marry him, ownership would transfer to him. Colton didn't care for the hard work involved in running the ranch, that's what the less fortunate were for. What he did care about was that he was going to be one of the richest ranchers in the country.

His dreams were dashed, however, when he saw his intended in the arms of another. And to make things worse, the man was only a ranch hand. Had he been another rancher or even a rancher's son, he could have forgiven Nitika for being taken in by his charm. But a broken-down cowboy was more than he could stand.

"Perhaps Tilton was taking advantage of a weak moment," he

muttered to himself as the train began to ascend a steep grade. "Why else would she allow herself to stoop that low?"

The man across from Colton looked over his paper at him. Seeing that he wasn't talking anymore, the man assumed he was talking to himself and went back to his paper. Colton never noticed the attention he was getting with his ruminations. If he could get rid of the foreman, Nitika would have no choice but to come to him for support. His problem now was figuring out just how to get Hunter out of the way.

Having him killed would only turn Nitika away from him if she ever found out. He could have him kidnapped and turned loose only after he convinced Nitika to marry him. Colton shook his head, again Nitika could find out he was behind it. No, Hunter would have to leave on his own if he wanted a chance with Nitika. Maybe he could somehow threaten the man. Perhaps something in Hunter's past would force him to leave. But how could he find such dirt on a man he didn't even know?

The Pinkerton Detective Agency was located in Chicago. When he got home, he was going to give them a visit and see if they had an agent they could send in. With that settled, Colton leaned back in his seat completely pleased with his plan. Nitika would be his in no time.

Hunter pulled a small trunk from under his bed. From the very bottom of it, he dug out a small box. Inside was the ring he was going to give to Irena. They had been so in love back then. But Irena changed all that and he was forced to join the army. To this day, his father still believed the girl over him. If Nitika ever heard about it, she'd never forgive him.

Putting the box back in its hiding place, Hunter quickly dressed and ran down to the dining hall. With Colton Dagon gone, things were back to normal. He didn't even mind the good-natured ribbing from the men as they ate breakfast. Nitika wasn't exactly hiding her feelings for him either. Hunter felt that if the other men weren't in the room, she'd be sitting on his lap.

Dyami looked between his daughter and Hunter and grinned. He felt sure they'd be hearing wedding bells soon. When his surprise for Nitika arrived, it could be any day now. The king size bed he ordered for her room should give her the idea that he didn't want to wait to be a grandfather. He wanted to be young enough to enjoy any grandchildren she would have.

But Nitika had a mind of her own and would marry when she was ready. A wedding would bring up another problem, though. Odelia. Nitika's mother would most likely show up and Dyami didn't know if that was a good thing or not. It was clear that Nitika and Odelia weren't exactly close. Who knew what would happen if things didn't go Odelia's way. Then there was the thought of seeing his ex-wife again, especially looking like he did.

"What's wrong, Father," Nitika asked touching his arm.

He smiled at her. "Nothing," he said patting her hand. "Why do you ask?"

"You were deep in thought and it didn't look like it was a pleasant thought."

"When you go into town today, I'd like you to take a letter to Darren Castle."

"The lawyer? Why? What's going on?"

"You ask too many questions. Everything's fine. I just want him to check on something for me."

Nitika nodded, but she didn't believe her father. Something was on his mind and it was bothering him. She only hoped he wasn't sending the lawyer a will for him to register. Uncle Alex had his done just before the drive that killed him. The Oldriches were locked away in jail and no one else wanted their land at the moment. What else would he need the help of a lawyer for? Maybe he was checking to make sure the ranch was legally hers.

Dandy hooked up the team while Dyami wrote his letter. He wanted to know for sure if he was married to Odelia or not. More for her sake than his own. He didn't mind the single life so much now. Most of the women he met since the accident had either been appalled or overly sympathetic by his appearance. There had only been maybe two who didn't care what he looked like, but one of them didn't really count. Violet Panner was a blind saloon owner who gave him a job for about a month when he was looking for Nitika.

The other woman was the Kiowa maiden who nursed him back to health. Dyami thought about Sakari Tala, Sweet Wolf, from time to time. She had been heartbroken when he told her he was leaving. In a way, he wished he could have taken her with him. But not knowing if he was still married, it wouldn't have been right to the girl to take her away from her family like that. Perhaps once things were settled with Odelia, he'd go find her and bring her to the ranch. That is, if she hadn't already married another.

Chapter 4

Nitika kept staring at the letter in her hand. What didn't her father want her to know about? He had written the letter and sealed it shut with a wax seal. Was he just testing her or was it really a very important matter? Dandy chuckled at her.

"I don't think your father would keep anything that important a secret from you."

"Then why won't he tell me?"

"Maybe it's a surprise and he doesn't you want to spoil it."

"What kind of a surprise could involve a lawyer?"

"I don't know, maybe a wedding present for you and Hunter." Nitika snorted and Dandy laughed at her. "Come on, he's not that bad of a man. He's crazy in love with you."

Nitika looked at Dandy and waited for one of the insults he was known for, but it didn't come. "What makes you think he'll ask me?"

"Ma'am, I've seen the way he looks at you."

"Oh, and just how does Hunter look at me," she asked haughtily.

"Like he wants to devour you. I've never seen a man that in love with a woman before. Makes me wonder if he's not touched in the head."

"Careful, Dandy. I'm the one who pays your money."

"I don't mean it like that, Ma'am. Maybe if you two were married, he wouldn't get all cow-eyed whenever he sees you."

"So you're saying I'm keeping Hunter from doing his job?"

Dandy looked over at her defensive posture. "I'm going to shut up now Ma'am, before I get myself in more trouble."

"Smart move," she said as the town came into view.

Nitika went straight to the lawyer's office to deliver her father's letter. Depending on what it was for, Mr. Castle might have an answer to take back with her. She didn't know how urgent it was. But it was important enough that he sent it in now instead of when he came into town next. She waited in the outer office while he read the letter.

"Tell your father I will have an answer for him soon," Castle said. "I have to consult a few of my books first."

Nitika stalled as long as she could before deciding it was time to head for home. She was really worried about what her father wanted with a lawyer. Dandy was patiently waiting for her on the buckboard. With a sigh, she climbed up onto the seat beside him. The freight line owner waved them down as they passed by his store.

"I've got a crate here for your father Miss Brodie. You think you have room for it?"

Nitika looked at the half-filled buckboard. "It depends on how big it is. What is it?"

"The order says it's a bed. King-sized I'd guess from the size of the crate," the man said looking at the paper in his hand.

Dandy wrapped the reins around the brake. "Maybe we can take it out of the crate. I'm sure the pieces will fit somewhere."

"Why did Father buy a new bed," she wondered out loud.

"There you go suspecting your father again," Dandy muttered climbing down.

Between Dandy and two freight workers, they managed to get the new bed complete with mattress in the buckboard and strapped down. Nitika was quiet on the way home as she pondered her father's reasoning for buying such a large bed. Dandy continued to protest her curiosity at her father's actions. Dyami was coming from the stable as they pulled up to the main house.

17

"I was hoping the freighting office would deliver that," he said seeing the mattress holding everything down.

"Why did you buy the bed," Nitika asked before he could say anything else.

"I thought since you own the ranch, you deserved a bigger bed to sleep on," he said innocently. "Especially if you decide to marry sometime. Your husband wouldn't like sleeping on that small bed of yours."

"I'm guessing you'd like it to be sooner rather than later, right Father?"

Dyami smiled at her. "I never could pull anything over on you, could I?"

With Anna carrying the linens, they managed to switch beds before Anna had to cook supper. Nitika waited until she was alone to test out the bed. Hunter found her spread eagle in the middle of the thick mattress. With the knowing look Dyami gave him when he was sent up here, he knew the meaning of the new bed as well.

"Got good strong ropes on it," he asked Nitika.

Nitika bolted straight up, embarrassed he caught her acting like a little girl. "Why? You think you're going to get to try them out?"

"Your father *is* pushing pretty hard for us to get married."

"Maybe it's because he isn't. Or at least, he can't go home to Mother. She'd never accept him looking like he does."

"Does it bother you too," he asked reading the frown on her face.

"Sometimes, but not like how you think," she said quickly. "There are times when I see his good side and forget about his left side. Then when he turns, it catches me off guard and I wish the accident never happened. But I still love him the same now as I did before. Mother would never look at him the same again."

"Anna said supper's almost ready. And I have a feeling if we aren't down there soon, they might think we're testing out the bed."

The lawyer showed up at the ranch a couple days later carrying some books and papers. Nitika tried to join her father in the study, but he locked the door. She put her ear to the door. But the thick wood blocked any sound that might carry. Looking in the windows wouldn't help either since he pulled the curtains closed.

"Why all the secrecy Mr. Brodie," Castle asked as Dyami closed the curtains.

"I don't want Nitika to know what's going on until I know for sure if I'm still married to Odelia."

"Is she hoping that you and your wife will reconcile?"

"No. She knows there's no hope of that. Odelia has found another man. If she's plans on marrying this man, I don't want it to be illegal."

"Well, I wired a friend of mine in Richmond. He looked into the records there. According to court documents, Odelia had your marriage annulled after you were declared dead. I guess she didn't want to have any doubt that you were no longer married. Now, I've asked him to send me a copy of the annulment. It should be here in a couple weeks."

"I would say her reason for annulling the marriage is that she didn't want to own half the ranch. She never liked it out here. Too remote for her."

Darren Castle nodded but didn't say a word. Why a woman wouldn't want half of this ranch, he didn't know. Alexander Brodie had built it into a very lucrative business. He only hoped that Nitika could continue that success. Looking at the improvements that she had made since inheriting the D Bar A Ranch, he knew she was more than capable of running it, but not a lot of men liked to deal with women. If she only had a husband to help her, who knows how far she could go.

"Well, I will bring you those papers when I get them," Castle said gathering up his papers.

"You didn't tell your friend who was asking about Odelia, did you," Dyami asked expectantly.

"I told him that I was finalizing the ownership and needed to know if she had any legal ties to it."

"If she finds out, she'll think Nitika put you up to it. I hate doing that to her, but it can't be helped. Nitika will understand."

Chapter 5

William Pinkerton looked across his desk at the young man. Colton Dagon looked like a very anxious person. He fidgeted in his seat, twisting his hat around in his hand. Knowing who was involved, William knew why the man was sitting here instead of in his father's office. Dagon was trying to horn in on Nitika Brodie's life. He had read the reports from Nitika on her field work for the company. The girl was very good and she would know a set up sooner than either one of them could anticipate. But the kind of money that Colton was offering was enough for him to seriously consider taking the job.

"What you're asking of us is very sensitive. I will have to think on it some. Miss Brodie does know several of our best agents. It will be hard to find men that won't talk to these men. They have a way of getting what they want out of people. Give me until the end of the week to give you an answer."

"I understand your reluctance," Colton said seething inwardly. "Miss Brodie does have quite a lot of influence in her region. A scandal could damage her reputation as well as hurt the ranch business. Neither of which I want to happen."

William had the feeling that Dagon was more concerned about

Nitika's money than he was about her. He could tell the man was ambitious and that took money. It was something that Colton didn't have an abundance of just yet. But if William did his job right, he was being guaranteed a portion of Dagon's share of the ranch.

"Until the end of the week then," William said dismissing him.

Colton stood and placed his hat on his head. "Until then."

He let his emotions show once he was out of sight of the Pinkerton office. How could any man turn down what he was offering? Most men he knew would take a ten percent interest in a rich ranch like the D Bar A without hesitation. Colton had gone to William when Allan turned him down. That was something else he couldn't understand either. Pinkerton was not known for turning down money.

Colton hailed a hack to take him back to his parents' house. He had taken a room at the Grand Hotel and wanted to pick up some of his things. He had cleaned out his apartment and was storing his possessions at his parents' place. The apartment he had been renting was no longer suitable for a man of his future status. Hopefully by the end of the month, he would be moving out west to be with his new wife, or rather bringing her here.

Brady Huntington was overseeing the latest shipment of goods being loaded for the long trek west when two men approached him. He gave the order to his second in command to finish while he dealt with them. Straightening his tie, he went to greet the newcomers.

"Good day Gentlemen. What can I do for you today?"

"Are you Brady Huntington," the one asked.

"Why yes I am. What can I do for you?"

The other man looked around. "Is there some place we can talk privately?"

Brady swept a hand toward his Savannah office. "My office is this way. May I ask what this is about?"

"We'd rather not say out here," the second man said.

After offering the men a drink, Brady settled in his chair behind the desk. "Now, what is all this secrecy about? Why are you here?"

"Do you have a son by the same name as yours?"

"Can I ask who you are first," Brady asked annoyed by the men's rudeness.

"Thomas Wilks and Charles Dolby, Pinkerton agents," Thomas said showing his badge.

"Why are you asking me about my son? I haven't seen him in years."

"It has come to our attention that Brady Huntington Jr has been keeping company with a very wealthy, unmarried young woman. A woman who is the intended of one of our clients."

"What is it you want me to do? We haven't spoken in years. By now, he is old enough to make his own mistakes. Besides, he stopped listening to me years ago."

"Mr. Huntington," Charles said, "we are aware of your son's prior activities. We know why you made him join the army. We also know about what he's done since his discharge. Our client has hired us to find a way to get your son away from his fiancé. If you can't somehow convince him to leave the girl, we will be forced to use other methods."

"What other methods," Brady asked narrowing his eyes.

"Your son has been involved in some questionable activities. Things you wouldn't want to be publicly known. You might lose a good deal of your business," Dolby said.

"Just what is it you think my son has done," he asked suspiciously.

"We'd rather not say at this moment," Wilks said with a smug look on his face.

"I can certainly try, but he's a stubborn one. Got that from his mother. Where is my son living at right now?"

"Sante Fe New Mexico," Wilks said. "Won't be hard to find. It's the largest cattle ranch in the territory."

"I've got a train headed that way next week. Probably take the better part of a month getting there."

Wilks looked at Dolby. "Our client is getting rather nervous now. It's taken us almost that long already to find you. He feels that the longer your son is in his woman's life, the harder it will be to get him to leave."

"Why doesn't this client of yours fight for this girl if he really wants her?"

"Our client isn't a fighting man Mr. Huntington. He's afraid that if he braces your son, he's the one who will end up dead. Besides, if he should best your son, his woman will never forgive him and not marry him. He feels that it would best for everyone if your son left of his own free will, given the right circumstances."

"Yeah," Brady said scratching his chin. "I see what you're getting at. You'll have to give me give a few days to get things in order here. I can't just pack up and go when I please. I've got a business to run here."

"We understand Mr. Huntington. Our train leaves in two days. We'll be expecting you then," Wilks said as they left.

What am I doing, Hunter wondered as he laid flat on his back looking up at the blue sky through the haze of dust. He and four others were checking cows to see how many might be bred. Right now, they were hazing Old Red Nose's girls out of the woods. Someone had to keep the bull busy while the others checked the cows. Hunter drew the short straw which meant he was the one to distract him.

He felt hot breath on his face and knew Red Nose was standing above him. Hunter quickly scrambled to his feet and ran for his horse. Forking the saddle on the run, he made a frantic grab for the stirrups. He barely planted his feet firm, when Red Nose raked his mount with a horn. The frightened animal shrieked and began bucking.

Hunter managed to get him under control as the bull made another charge at him. This time, he managed to get a horn under Hunter's leg and drag him from the saddle. Landing awkwardly, Hunter felt something tear in his shoulder. He heard a shot and Red Nose roar in pain. The massive animal turned on the cause of his agony.

Seeing Hunter in trouble, Colby took a shot at the bull. He meant to shoot over his head to scare him, but Red Nose moved just as Colby squeezed the trigger. The bullet grazed the bull's left flank. Dandy skirted the angry monster and gave Hunter a hand up onto his horse. He then rode after Hunter's frightened mount.

"You alright," Dandy asked as they watched Colby outrun Red Nose.

"Yeah," Hunter said a little out of breath. "I'm beginning to think that Nitika should get rid of him. He's too dangerous."

"Well, he has been around a long time. Maybe that was part of her plan when she brought him closer to the other cattle. Besides, you're the one who almost got killed out there. She's bound to do something now."

"I hardly think she'll get rid of him because of me," Hunter said swinging into his own saddle.

"Good foremen are hard to come by. She'll be hard pressed to replace you."

"Funny, Dandy. Come on. We still got a couple pastures to check before supper."

Chapter 6

Nitika had her sleeves rolled up, pulling weeds from her vegetable garden when she heard the buggy. She recognized the livery's rented horse and wondered who would be coming out to the ranch. The man holding the reins looked uncomfortable bouncing along the trail to the house. His clothes spoke of money and Nitika became wary. The last person she saw who looked like that had tried to steal her ranch.

She continued her weeding as her father came from the barn, still holding the harness he was repairing. The buggy came to a stop in front of the house. The man stepped down and walked over to her. He waited for her to look up at him. Too good to talk to the hired help, she thought, dusting her hands off on her jeans.

"Something I can do for you," she asked standing up.

"You can tell me where I can find the owner of this ranch," he said haughtily.

Nitika bit her tongue to keep her comments to herself. "You're looking at her. What can I do for you?"

Brady Huntington looked unbelieving at the young woman in front of him. "You own this ranch? You're Nitika Brodie?"

"That's right. You have a problem with that?"

Dyami started for the house when he saw Nitika take a defensive stance. She saw him moving and held up her hand. He stopped where he was, Nitika wanted to handle this on her own. If she got in trouble, she knew he'd step in. Brady saw the ranch hand obey the command and knew the dirt covered woman in front of him was Nitika Brodie.

"My name is Brady Huntington. I was told that my son is working here. I've come to take him home."

"Sorry, but I don't have anyone by the name of Huntington working here. Whoever told you that is wrong."

Huntington frowned. "The Pinkertons assured me that he was here. They rarely make a mistake. Maybe he gave you a false name."

"Possible. What's he look like," Nitika asked stepping out of the garden.

"He's about twenty five, tall, dark hair and blue eyes. Favors his mother in looks."

Nitika looked closer at Brady Huntington. "What's her maiden name?"

"Tilton, why?"

"What's your son's name?"

"Brady Huntington II. What's with all the questions? Does my son work here or not?"

"He works here. Goes by the name of Hunter Tilton, though. He's my foreman."

Hunter was tired and hurting by the time their work was done. He couldn't wait to get back to the house. Thoughts of Nitika rubbing liniment on his sore muscles made the fight with Red Nose almost seem worth it. Colby saw the grin on his face and slapped him on the shoulder.

"Wish I had me a woman that'd make me smile like that," he said riding out of range.

"Last I heard, you had about six fawning over you," Hunter retorted.

"Yeah, but they ain't the rancher's wife kind. You got a rare one in Miss Brodie."

Hunter heard the longing in Colby's voice. Despite his bravado and carefree attitude, he really did want a place of his own with a woman who wanted the same thing. He could smell supper cooking as the hands headed for the back door to wash up. As normal, he bypassed the back porch and went into the house. Since moving into the main house, he was treated as a member of the family. One of these days, he planned on making it official. He was just waiting for the right moment.

He heard voices coming from the parlor as he headed for his room. Walking past the stairs, he looked into the room. Nitika had an older gentleman caller she didn't look too happy to be talking to. She looked up when he stepped into the doorway. The man turned around to see who entered the room.

"Hello Son," Brady said.

"What are you doing here, Father," Hunter asked suspiciously.

"I came to ask you to come home."

Hunter went over and stood beside Nitika. "You came a long way for nothing then. I'm not going back with you."

"Son, I need help with the business."

"What about Thomas or Evan? Why can't they help out?"

Brady shook his head. "Your brothers aren't exactly the business type. Besides, your mother misses you."

"And who's fault was that? You're the one who made me join the army to avoid-." Hunter paused. Nitika knew nothing about his life before they met. What would she think about him if she knew everything?

"Son, it's only right for you to take over. You are the oldest after all."

"What do you mean 'take over'?"

"I'm dying Son. The doctor says I only have a few months to live."

Hunter shook his head. "No. This is some kind of trick. I told you years ago I would never set foot in your house again. What's the real reason you're here?"

"It's the truth Son. I need you to come back to keep the business going, for your mother's sake. She won't survive without it and you know how women are in business. They can't handle it the way men do."

Hunter squeezed Nitika's shoulder to keep her from speaking up. From looking at the ledgers, he knew that she had already increased the profits here at the ranch. And from the way she was going, she was looking at doubling her worth in a year or so. But what his father said was true about his mother. She knew nothing about the freighting business and could easily lose it.

"Supper's ready," Anna said from the door.

She had set four places at the table in the kitchen to give them privacy from the hands. Given how Mr. Huntington had acted earlier, Anna knew the man would make things more difficult if he was made to eat with the hired help. Dyami came in, still dripping wet from dunking his head in the water trough and grabbed the coffee pot. Brady scoffed at the boldness of this one ranch hand.

"Who's our guest Nitika," he asked joining them at the table.

"This is Brady Huntington, Father. He's Hunter's father."

Dyami only nodded. Hunter didn't look happy to have his father here, he thought. The meal was a silent affair as no one felt like talking. He could feel the stares from Huntington, but ignored them. Since the accident, he was used to people staring at him. The man had seemed surprised when Nitika had addressed him. It was obvious, Brady didn't think rich people worked hard enough to get dirty.

Dyami declined joining them in the parlor afterwards. He was getting ready to take a trip and still had some more packing to do. He was going to search for Sweet Wolf. Now that he knew he wasn't married, he wanted to find out how she really felt about him. And if possible, bring her home as his wife.

Nitika heard Hunter groan as he sat on the couch. She had seen him holding his arm close to his side all evening. Something had happened out on the range, but he didn't want her to know. Or perhaps he was keeping it from his father. Excusing herself, Nitika went to the kitchen to bring coffee to the parlor. Hunter rubbed the sleep from his eyes and his father gave him a disapproving look.

Chapter 7

"The least you could do would be to stay awake while I'm here," he growled.

"I've had a very long day that started very early this morning. And I have another one again tomorrow. I'm sorry if you don't approve of my choice of jobs, but it's what I like to do."

"Is it the job or the owner that you like?"

"What does Nitika have to do with this?"

Brady gave a knowing nod. "So, it's happening again I see. I thought you learned your lesson the last time Son."

"What lesson? What are you talking about?" Hunter thought for a minute. "You're talking about Irena, aren't you? No, it can't be. We never did anything."

Brady stood up and glared at his son. "You most certainly did do something. That girl had to leave to have your child."

"Father, I never slept with Irena. I told you that years ago. You didn't listen then either. So there's no point in bringing up the past."

"She told her father it was yours. Galvin threatened to have you thrown in jail if you didn't take responsibility for your actions. That's why I made you join the army, to get away from the man. Why would the girl lie?"

"Maybe because you own the largest shipping company in Georgia instead of the local market. Irena probably thought I'd have to marry her if she said it was mine instead of Tommy Roberts."

"But you were going to marry her," Brady said meekly. "Why did she go and fool around with that little whelp?"

"I don't know. Maybe because I refused her advances once and she wanted to get back at me. After I found out she was with Tommy, I was ready to break it off. But then she comes up with the story that she's carrying my child. Next thing I know, you're shipping me off to parts unknown."

"Yes well, she wasn't the only woman you've been with. I know about that little tart down in Texas. Her father was determined to kill you when he found out about the two of you."

"And how would he know that? We never told anyone. How do you even know?"

"I had you followed for a while after you joined. I wanted to make sure you were safe. But the detective told me he caught you with a girl from a very rich family. I didn't want another incident like back home so I convinced the girl to leave."

Hunter lunged to his feet. "You've meddled in my life long enough. Nitika and I are none of your concern. As far as the business goes, it can just go under."

With that said, Hunter stormed from the room. He passed Nitika carrying a tray to the parlor on the way to his old quarters. Throwing the dust cover off his bed, he flopped down on the mattress. The motion sent fresh pain through his injured shoulder and he tried to rub it. His anger at his father deepened the more he thought about what his father had done to him.

His front door opened and Nitika walked in. Hunter saw the jar of liniment in her hand as she closed the door behind her. "I know this hasn't been a pleasant visit for you and your father."

"I just can't believe what he's done to me on the word of one woman," he said unbuttoning his shirt.

"It's amazing what some people will do to save face," she said crawling onto the bed behind him. "Red Nose give you a lot of trouble?"

He jerked away from her when she touched the tender muscles. "Yeah. Dandy thinks he's getting to be too dangerous to keep."

"Feels like you pulled a muscle," she said running her fingers gently down the sore spot.

Hunter only nodded to keep from letting her know how bad it hurt. He soon felt the heat of the lotion and gave himself over to the massage. Nitika avoided the bruises she saw as she worked across his shoulders.

"Well after he breeds all his ladies, I planned on selling him anyhow. I don't need to be patching you, or anyone else, up because of him."

He felt himself falling forward, but Nitika caught him. "Why don't you lay down before I have to pick you up off the floor?"

Nitika continued to work over his aching body until he fell asleep. She rubbed more liniment onto his injury. If it still hurt him in the morning, she was going to get Doc to look at it. It bothered her that she was going to have to get rid of her best stud, but the safety of her men was more important. Brady Huntington was sitting on her front porch when she returned.

"Mr. Huntington. I thought you were going to bed."

"Don't think I don't know what's going on Missy," he groused.

"And just what do you think is going on," she asked crossing her arms across her chest.

"I saw you coming from my son's quarters. Does your father know what you're doing behind his back?"

"He knows. Hunter had been sleeping upstairs in his own room instead of that cabin for the past month. Father also knows that we're old enough to make our own decisions."

"Do you love my son?"

"Very much so. And I think he feels the same way."

"I'm sorry to hear that. It's going to make his leaving that much more painful. For both of you."

"You seem so sure he's going to leave me to go home with you."

"He is my oldest son. He knows it's his responsibility to take over the business."

"Despite whether he's happy or not, is that it?"

"Happiness has nothing to do with family obligation. Brady will come home with me and take his rightful place."

"Maybe, but are you willing to lose everything else in the process?"

Nitika left him there to think as she went into the house. Brady didn't like what came to mind. His son never did like working in the office. He preferred the outdoors to city life. It was beginning to look like if Brady got his hands on the business, he'd sell out and move back here. And that was something that Brady, the elder, didn't want to happen.

Hunter stared up at the ceiling long after the breakfast bell rang. How was he going to tell the men he was leaving? They all had their minds made up that he was going to marry Nitika. In fact, he was even thinking it himself lately. But his father's health was more important right now. If it gave his father peace of mind for him to go home with him, then Hunter would agree to it. After his father was gone, he could do what he pleased with the freighting business.

But it could take a year or more to accomplish what he wanted. Would Nitika wait for him that long? Somehow he doubted a beautiful woman like her would be able to hold out. Some other man would come along and sweep her off her feet. No, she'd most likely be married with a baby by the time he could come back for her.

The mood was somber when he finally made it to the dining room. Hunter wondered if Nitika already told them he was leaving. He caught the smug look on his father's face and knew who told the men. Anger boiled to the surface, but Hunter forced himself to remain calm. He didn't want to give his father the satisfaction of ragging him.

"I take it you've all heard," he said looking at the men.

Chapter 8

"Ain't heard it from you, Boss," Doc said stabbing at another steak.

"You've all met my father by now, I'm sure. He's not in the best of health and he's asked me to go home and run the family business."

"You going," Dandy asked looking at Nitika.

"I don't have a choice Dandy. I'm needed at home."

"What kind of a business is it," Colby asked.

"It's a freighting company. Huntington Freighting out of Savannah Georgia."

"At least we know you ain't after Miss Brodie's money," Colby joked. "Why didn't you ever tell us that before?"

"For the same reason Doc didn't tell us he was a real doctor. It wasn't something I wanted to talk about."

"How soon will you be leaving," Nitika asked quietly.

"My train leaves in three days," Brady said toying with the food on his plate. "I expect Junior to be on it with me."

Nitika saw Hunter's jaw working. He obviously didn't like being called Junior. She saw him wince as he sat down beside her. Something didn't feel right about this situation. Brady Huntington didn't look or act like a man who was dying. He said that the Pinkertons had found

Hunter for him. Perhaps she needed to take a little trip herself to find out for sure.

Dyami came into the room and kissed her cheek. He was carrying his saddlebags. His horses were packed for his secret trip. What was he up to, she wondered for the thousandth time. Her father had been very secretive for the past month or so. What was it he didn't want her to know about? She walked with him outside.

"I hope to be back in a month or two Angel."

"Why won't you tell me what this is all about? I have connections that might help you with whatever."

Dyami smiled. "Sorry Sweetheart. I don't think you know the right people for what I'm doing. It's nothing for you to worry about, I promise."

Doc came out as Dyami was riding away. "Still won't tell you, will he?"

"No. Has he said anything to you?"

"Sorry Darling. Mr. Brodie hasn't told anyone anything. You really going to let him go?"

"Who? Hunter?"

"Of course I mean Hunter," he chuckled. "No one else has got their rope around you, have they?"

"I don't have a say in this Doc. I can't compete against a dying father. If he really is dying."

"You think it's a trick? Why would a man lie about dying?"

"I don't know. But you'd think a man who doesn't have long to live would try to make amends with his son. Especially if he wants him to take over a business."

"You got a point Darling, but how do you prove it?"

"By taking a little trip."

"Now hold on there Girl. With your father gone and Hunter leaving, who's going to be in charge if you leave?"

She looked at him and smiled. Doc put his hands up in protest. "Don't you go looking at me like that. I don't know the first thing about running a ranch."

"Doc, you've been here longer than anyone else. I only plan on being gone a couple days. Surely you can keep a lid on things for that long."

"Only a couple days," he asked hesitantly.

"This trip, yes"

Doc's mouth gaped open. "You mean there's going to be more?"

"I don't know for sure. I'll know more after this one."

Hunter shifted his arm in the sling again as they waited for the train to arrive. Doc had told him not to use his arm for a couple days after pulling a muscle. True to her word, Nitika sold the old bull to a neighboring ranch once she knew her cows were bred. Now, she stood by his side dry-eyed, losing something else she cared about. What tears she would shed would be done in the privacy of her room where no one could see them, that much he knew.

Brady was snapping orders at the porters caring for his luggage. Hunter was embarrassed by the scene his father was making. He apparently had forgotten where he himself had come from to be treating the working class as he did. Picking up his war bag, Hunter followed his father on board.

"Honestly, Son. Surely you have more than just that tattered old bag. It's an embarrassment for me to see you looking like a tramp."

"Then I guess you won't mind if I don't sit with you," he ground out.

Hunter pushed past his father and entered the coach car. He dropped his bag on a seat and sat across from it. Propping his feet up on it, he tried to get some sleep. An hour later, he felt someone tapping on his foot. He pushed his hat up and saw his father.

"I'm sorry Son. I don't know what came over me. Please, come back to the compartment. There's a lot we need to talk about."

Colby was fiddling with the reins of his horse while he stood beside Nitika. "You never told Hunter, did you?"

"What was there to say? I don't know what I'm going to find out in Chicago. His father could very well have hired Pinkerton to find him. And if he did, what would Hunter think about me then?"

"I guess you're right. But leaving Doc in charge? You sure that's a good idea?"

"Colby, I'm only going to be gone a couple days. Doc will do fine for that long."

"I hope you're right," Colby said pulling Nitika's carpetbag out from under the blankets in the buggy. "Your train's coming. Good luck, Ma'am."

Nitika entered the main office of the Pinkerton Detective Agency. The mousy receptionist recognized her and went to Allan's office. She showed the part-time detective into his office right away. Nitika sat down across from him as he finished putting the latest folders in his file cabinet. Allan swivelled around to face her, uncertainty on his face.

"This is a pleasant surprise, Miss Brodie. What brings you to my office?"

"Has a Brady Huntington from Georgia ever contacted you about finding his son?"

Allan pursed his lips in thought. "About five years ago, I recall a man looking for his son by that name. Let me go look it up."

Allan left the office and went into another room that was filled with old case files. He returned about twenty minutes later with several folders. Laying them out, he scanned through them quickly. "Here it is," he said pointing to one line. "Mr. Huntington was wanting to find where his son had gotten to after leaving the army. My operative found him engaged in a relationship with a young woman. Then I have another one here that shows Brady Jr. hiring out his gun to fight in a range war. Several others here have the boy hiring out his gun some more. But that's all I have. Why do you want to know?"

"Were all the files from back then? Nothing new?"

"Not that I have. My sons have their own files. You might want to ask them if they know Mr. Huntington. Why all the questions, my dear?"

"I have reason to believe a friend of mine has been set up. He's had to leave his life in order to care for an ailing father, who I don't believe is sick."

"What makes you think the father is faking his illness?"

"He's not acting like a dying man."

"How so, Miss Brodie?"

"If you were on the outs with one of your sons, would you not try to make amends with him instead of pushing him farther away? Especially if you want him to take over the family business?"

Chapter 9

"Why didn't you go to your friend with your suspicions?"

"Because I don't have any proof of this, yet. And if I'm wrong, I don't want to lose his friendship because of it. I'd rather not burn that bridge right now."

Allan grinned. "I knew there was a reason I hired you. Not many women think things through like you do. William is in his office now if you want to talk to him."

Nitika walked to the door and opened it. She quickly closed it before Colton Dagon saw her. Keeping it open a crack, she watched Colton talk with William before leaving. Allan came up behind her and peered out of the door as well. He growled when he saw the man leaving his son's office.

"I'm beginning to think this is a setup for your friend. Or I should say your foreman."

"Colton come to see you?"

"A while ago. He was wanting me to dig up some dirt on your foreman that would make him leave. My guess is the snake wanted to get his fangs in you."

"He has, ever since my father willed his half of the ranch to me.

He came out to my place trying to convince me to marry him. When he saw Hunter and me together, he got angry. I should have known he would stoop this low."

Once Colton was out of sight, Nitika walked over to William's office. As she reached for the door, the receptionist tried to stop her. William looked up when he heard all the commotion outside his door. He frowned when he saw who it was, followed by his father.

"Hello William. Surprised to see me," Nitika asked.

"What brings you to Chicago?"

"From what I just saw, you brought me here. What was Colton Dagon doing here?"

"I don't have to tell you anything," he said indignantly.

"Maybe not her, but you have to tell me," Allan said.

"Mr. Dagon wanted me to find some way of getting rid of your foreman. He claimed you were engaged and that your foreman was standing in the way of you getting married."

"Being engaged means actually accepting the proposal," Nitika said walking up to his desk. "How much was he going to pay you for your services?"

"That is none of your business," William said crossing his arms across his chest.

"How much," she screamed pounding on his desk.

William reached out to catch the lamp that threatened to fall from her tirade. His father frowned at him. He almost laughed at the thought that came to him. He was more afraid of the girl than he was of his father.

"You are looking at being fired if you don't answer her Son. She is part Indian and you might just wake up that side of her."

"He promised me a ten percent cut of the value of your ranch once you were married," he finally said.

Nitika smiled. "He would have made you a wealthy man. Too bad I never would have married him."

"Why did you agree to work for him when you knew Miss Brodie was involved? You knew she worked for us on several occasions. You also know she doesn't give up anything very easily. I even told you how much she loved her foreman. Did you really think she would let him go without a fight?"

"I was thinking about the money it would bring in. You would have done the same thing if he'd come to you," he protested.

"I turned him down flat, Son. I wasn't about to betray a friend like that. She's better off on our side. What do you plan to do now, my dear?"

"I don't know just yet. My father's left on a secret mission of his own and I don't have a new foreman. I need to find a manager to take care of the place before I think about going to Savannah. Do you know of anyone?"

"Well, your men know Devon and Raven. Devon was foreman on a couple ranches before coming to work for me. They've both played foreman when I needed them to. I have a feeling that Raven would like another crack at that wrangler of yours."

"Doc will be thrilled to have the 'young pup' back on the ranch. Making him boss would only make things worse. But I'd be glad to have them if they aren't working right now. At least I know I can trust them."

"They're due back from vacation any day now. Soon as they get here, I'll send them your way. And you," Allan said turning on his son, "are not to say a word to Mr. Dagon about this conversation. If I find out he gets wind of this, it's your head I'll take."

"Yes Sir," William ground out.

Colton whistled a tune as he walked down Main Street. His meeting with William Pinkerton went well. A report from the detectives in Savannah said that Hunter had come home to take care of his "ailing" father. What surprised him was that the former foreman came from a rich family. From the way he was living, Colton had felt sure the man was poor. He was curious about why Hunter never said anything about being a Huntington.

He got a feeling that he was being followed and turned around to look. With the crowd of people, it was hard to tell if anyone was tailing him. Colton continued his walk still feeling like he was being watched. Looking in store front windows, he tried to see around him. Nothing and no one looked out of place. It wasn't until he reached his hotel room that he felt safe.

Nitika saw the curtains move as Colton looked down on the street. He certainly was jumpy as he left the Pinkerton office. The more he squirmed, the more she liked it. She almost lost him once while she followed him from across the street. Colton had stopped in front of a leather goods store to adjust his tie. Knowing the real reason he stopped, Nitika had ducked into a general store to avoid being seen. A woman walked in front of her and she didn't see him continue on.

It wasn't hard for her to pick up his trail again as he rudely brushed past several couples. Now that she knew what hotel he was staying at, she could keep an eye on him for a couple days. If she recalled correctly, his parents lived in a small house at the edge of town. It was a far cry from the Grand Hotel he now stayed at. Could he possibly be thinking of using her money to pay for the extravagance? He had another thing coming if he thought that.

Nitika began shopping in the stores around the hotel waiting for Colton to show again. When he did, she shadowed him like before. She had him on edge, exactly the way she wanted him. He continually checked behind himself, but could never spot her. By the next day, he stayed hidden in his hotel room. Thoroughly spooked, it wasn't likely he'd leave any time soon. Satisfied, Nitika boarded the train for home.

She and Doc were going over plans for the swampy area in the eastern pasture when they saw two riders coming over the ridge. Doc growled when he recognized the black horse and rider. Nitika giggled when she saw who he was looking at.

"What are those two doing back here?"

"Allan sent them to take care of things while I go to Savannah to bring Hunter home."

"Never thought I'd see the day you'd go chasing after a man. Makes me think you're actually female."

"I ain't found one worth chasing until now Doc."

Chapter 10

Raven grinned when he saw who was talking to Nitika. Even from the ridge, he could see the man's disapproval. He knew why he and his partner were back on the D Bar A Ranch. There was no chance of winning the lady's fancy, he knew that now. Doc Hawkins had no reason to be wary of him. Nitika had chosen her man and no one was going to keep her from him.

"I don't want you antagonizing the man," Devon said, reading his partner's mind. "We are here to keep the ranch in one piece while the boss lady's away."

"What if he starts something? I'm not going to let it slide."

"No, I wouldn't expect you to. That's not your style." Raven opened his mouth to protest. "I know what you're going to say. You like to meet things head on. How Mr. Pinkerton ever thought we'd make good partners I'll never know. We are nothing alike."

Raven just growled and kept his mouth shut. They were riding into the yard by now and Nitika was walking over to the barn to meet them. Doc was hot on her heels, keeping himself between Raven and Nitika. He wasn't going to let the young Pinkerton detective near her.

"Allan tell you what this is about," she asked once they dismounted.

"Yeah," Devon said as Raven took his reins. "The story does sound a little off the wall. The detectives in Savannah are Thomas Wilks and Charles Dolby. They'd have been the ones who went to Huntington. They're just as money hungry as William is."

"Wilks will chase anything in a skirt. He'd be your best bet in breaking. Dolby is hen-pecked and doesn't care about other women," Raven added. "Afraid his wife will find out."

"Sounds like you've worked with them before."

"Once," Raven said. "They're good at their job, don't get me wrong. But they might smell a set up if you go at it wrong."

"You've never seen me work a skirt," Nitika said.

"And you're not going to see it now," Doc snapped.

"I've had just about enough of you Old Man," Raven said approaching the man.

"Doc," Nitika warned, "pull the horns in before I break them off. I will not have the two of you at each other's throats while I'm gone. Raven and Devon are here to help and you're just going to have to accept that."

"And that goes for you too, Partner. There's enough to do without the two of you going at it."

Doc and Raven glared at one another for a few more seconds before backing off. "Fine," Raven grated, "but this ain't over Old Man."

"It is until I get back," Nitika said, looking meaningful at both men.

The other hands rode in and saw the two Pinkerton agents. Worry etched their faces. The last time these men were here, Nitika and the others nearly got killed over the ranch. Nitika explained the reason for them coming back. While it eased some of the men, not all of them were convinced the agents were the best men for the job.

"Why not let Doc stay in charge," Dandy protested.

"Because Doc doesn't want to be in charge or I would. Do you want me to bring Hunter back or not?"

"Well yeah," Colby admitted. "He's the only one who's come close to marrying you. We don't want to lose him now."

"Alright," she said, blushing, "then you are going to have to take orders from Devon until either I or Father gets home."

"He might want to trade in them fancy duds of his for some real work clothes, though. Otherwise, they might get dirty," Dandy quipped.

Devon only chuckled. "At least *I* know how to impress the ladies."

The men almost didn't recognize Devon the next morning. Dressed in a plaid shirt and jeans, he looked more like a cowhand than the dude they were used to seeing. Raven took his time coming down for breakfast. Devon was about to call him on it when he saw Raven dragging a trunk with him. Nitika was behind him wearing a burgundy traveling suit.

"You pack fast Nitika," Devon said as Raven carried the trunk out to the waiting buggy.

"Not really, I've been packed since I came home. I was just waiting on you two to show up. The sooner I can solve this one, the quicker I'll have Hunter back."

"He must be worth it," Devon commented.

"I'll let you know when I bring him home."

Raven helped Nitika up onto the seat. Doc came out to see her off and frowned. That boy was going to be trouble. But they did call a truce while Nitika and her father were away. There was just something about Raven that rubbed him the wrong way. He just wished he could figure it out.

"Doc still has it in for me. You know that, don't you," Raven said once they left the ranch. "He still thinks I'm going to get between you and Hunter."

"He'll always think that. He's worse than an old woman when it comes to protecting me. Doc should know by now I can take care of myself."

"How long has he been here?"

"Ever since he got out of the army. Uncle Alex and Father bought the place just before he joined the army. Father took care of the place until Uncle Alex got out. He and Mother got married out here. They were at the ranch when I was born. Doc's was the first face I saw."

"Least I know where he's coming from."

"He really does mean well Raven. But yes, he is too protective."

Several men were eyeing Nitika as they waited for the train. She could feel their stares and was getting nervous. Though she tried not to let it show, Raven sensed her apprehension. When she went for a bite to eat, Raven approached the men.

"If you have any plans for that little lady, you'd better change them," he warned.

"Why," one of them asked. "What's she to you?"

"Not as much as I'd like. But I certainly don't want to get on her bad side again."

"Yeah," another sneered, "what happen the last time?"

"She broke my nose." Raven turned to leave, then paused. "By the way, she works for the Pinkertons. They protect their own."

He heard the men murmuring as he walked away. Raven only hoped he kept them from bothering Nitika. The girl was going to have enough trouble convincing her man that his father wasn't sick. If he wasn't working, he might have just looked up this Colton Dagon and settled with him. Nitika wasn't the kind of girl you got with deception. She was too smart for that.

When Nitika came back, the men quickly found interesting spots on the station walls to look at. She sat down beside a sleeping Raven and poked him in the ribs. He lifted his hat and looked sideways at her.

"Problem Miss Brodie," he asked.

"I can handle my own problems. I didn't need you to scare them off."

Raven grinned. "Nothing gets by you, does it? I know you can handle yourself, believe me," he said unconsciously rubbing his nose. "But sometimes it takes a man to do the job right. They didn't strike me as the type to leave a girl alone if *she* asked them."

Chapter 11

Dyami dismounted and ran his fingers through the dead fire pit. He felt a few warm coals still at the bottom. After so many cold fires, he was finally catching up with Sweet Wolf's tribe. Spending most of a year with them, he knew some of the route they took to get to their summer camping grounds. But finding their trail took some doing.

He was barely conscious when they first set out on their trek. By going to the scene of the explosion and making wide circles, Dyami was able to find their camp. After that, it was just a matter of following their trail. Rain and wind storms had blotted it out in places. Doggedly, he searched the area until he picked up their trail again.

Once he began to recognize a few landmarks, he started making better time. Now it seemed like he was only a day's ride behind them. With the growing dusk, he decided to make his camp here. Come tomorrow, he was determined to be at their campsite.

Emerging from the dense undergrowth, Dyami saw smoke circling toward the sky. The village was just down in the valley below him. His horse looked back at him when he hesitated. Would she have married by now? What if this trip was for nothing?

"What do you think Horse," he asked his mount.

His horse shook his head and pulled at the bit. He could smell water and wanted to get there sometime soon. He could also smell strange humans along with the water. That's why he didn't mind the wait. Taking a deep breath, Dyami nudged his mount forward.

Dogs and half naked children squealed and raced past him as he walked through the middle of the village. Several warriors gathered their weapons closer as they sat on their blankets. Not many men had the courage to boldly walk into their camp. They watched the man make his way over to Sweet Wolf's tent.

As he turned to dismount, they saw the scarred flesh on his face and knew who was calling on her. Dyami had returned as he had promised. The same warriors now rose and went to greet him. They silently cursed him for returning. Sweet Wolf had been giving up hope of seeing him again. They thought they might have a chance to marry her.

"It is good to see you again," one said reaching out his hand.

"Some how I don't believe you, Tall Tree," Dyami said with a grin as he took the man's hand. Tall Tree had been his biggest rival in vying for Sweet Wolf's affections.

"We did not recognize you when you first came in," Kajika added.

Hearing voices outside her tent, Sakari Tala pushed aside the door flap. She gasped when she recognized the man who was talking with her brothers' friends. Dyami turned when he heard her. He smiled when she ran to him, arms outstretched. Sweet Wolf buried her face in his shoulder as they embraced.

"I have missed you Dyami," she mumbled. "I knew you would come back."

"I don't break promises," he said as she pulled him toward her tent.

"Come, there is so much we have to talk about."

Dyami ducked through the low opening as she continued to pull his arm. He saw a papoose board leaning against the back wall. It sat empty and he wondered what had become of the baby. His question was answered when he saw a small bundle on Sweet Wolf's pallet moving. She saw where his gaze went and scurried over to her bed.

"This is your daughter, Awentia," she said, handing him the squirming bundle.

Dyami took the baby and looked down in her dark eyes. Fawn giggled and reached for the finger he extended to her. Sweet Wolf beamed as father and daughter met for the first time. Dyami sat down cross-legged and placed the baby on his lap.

"Are you sure she's mine," Dyami asked gently.

"Yes. You are the only man I have been with. Do you not believe me?"

Dyami heard the hurt in her voice. He hadn't meant it to sound like it did. But it had been a long time since he was last here. Many things could have happened by now. Sweet Wolf shuffled nervously in front of him waiting for an answer.

"Yes," he said looking up at her, "I do believe you. It has been many moons since we were last together. I did not know if you had married since I left."

"I wait for you," she said firmly. "You promised to come back and I wait. Did you find your family?"

"I found my daughter, but my brother had been killed in a stampede."

"I am sorry for you." She hesitated. "How did Nitika take this," she asked reaching for his face.

Dyami stopped her hand from touching him. "Nitika didn't care what I looked like. She only cared that I was alive."

"Does this mean you have come back to stay?"

Setting his daughter aside he motioned Sweet Wolf to sit. "That's why I came here to see you. I want to take you home with me."

She frowned. "But this is my home. My family is here. I do not want to leave them behind."

"I understand. My family is in New Mexico. I don't want to leave them behind either. I have already missed too much of my daughter's life."

48

"But she is grown," Sweet Wolf protested. "Fawn has much growing to do yet. Do you not want to see her grow?"

"Of course I do," Dyami said hesitantly. "But Nitika is old enough to make me a grandfather and I don't want to miss seeing my grandchildren."

"I will have to think about this," she said blinking back the tears. "Your world is not my world. I do not know that I will fit in with your people."

"I know that it will be a big change for you. That is why I am willing to wait for your answer. But I will not wait for a long time. I must get back to my family sometime."

"You will not think about staying here with me?"

"As you said, our worlds aren't the same. I would not be happy living here, so far from my world."

"Yet you want me to leave mine for yours."

"Your family is welcome to come see you anytime they wish. It would not work for mine to come here. There is much work to be done on a ranch that they could not visit."

"We could always go to them," she said hopeful.

"I would not be able to leave if we did. I love them too much to leave them like that."

"If I do not go with you, you would leave your daughter without a father?"

Dyami knew this question was coming and felt guilty about his answer. He knew that Sweet Wolf would be reluctant to leave the only life she knew. Walking away would have been easier if there wasn't a child involved. Yet, he knew that there were many young men who were willing to marry her should he not come back. In her own way, Sweet Wolf was sounding like Odelia. His former wife had also demanded he give up his life for the one she wanted him to have.

"As much as it pains me, yes I would leave our daughter fatherless."

Chapter 12

The day droned on for Hunter as he checked in another shipment. Lately, his days were running together. Monotony was setting in and it was driving him crazy. He secretly wished he could go with the shipment heading west just to see something other than the dock. His father shuffled up beside him and sighed.

Brady was getting weaker by the day. His clothes were ill fitting now and his face looked drawn. Still, he insisted on being at the docks every day. He nodded with satisfaction as another mule skinner left with his wagon laden down with goods heading for Colorado.

"I think I'm going to go home now, Son," he said before Hunter could say anything. "I just can't seem to make it all day anymore."

"It's okay. I can handle things here. You just go rest," Hunter said as another wagon pulled up to be loaded.

A stiff breeze blew the manifest from his hand as the wagon bumped against the dock. "Perfect," Hunter mumbled as he jumped down to retrieve the wayward papers. One began to take flight again as he reached out, but a woman stepped on it. He looked up and saw a familiar carpetbag. Straightening, he looked into the ebony eyes of Nitika.

"It's been a long time," she said.

"Too long," he sighed wrapping his arms around her. "What brings you out here?"

"You, of course." She began to smooth the lines on his face. "It hasn't been a good day, has it?"

Hunter released her and bent down to get the paper she was still standing on. "I haven't had one of those since I left the D Bar A."

Nitika didn't need to see his face to know how bad things had gotten. "How much more do you have to do?"

"This is my last wagon today. Once it's loaded, I'll be free the rest of the day, what's left of it."

"How about meeting me for dinner then? I'm staying at the Brenner House."

"I don't know how long I'll be here," Hunter said turning to the wagon.

"Alright," she said coming up behind him. "How about if you don't show, by say six o'clock, I'll eat alone."

Hunter had to repress a shudder of pleasure as her breath caressed the back of his neck. He silently nodded to keep from betraying his feelings about her to the mule skinner. The swish of her skirts caught not only his attention, but that of the driver as they both watched her leave. Seeing that he was being watched, the driver began to dust off his coat to avoid the scowl from Hunter.

"Your lady friend is quite the looker Mr. Huntington. If I was you, I'd get this wagon loaded so you could go be with her."

"That is none of your business," Hunter growled.

"All I'm saying is," the man said unphased by Hunter's mood, "if I had a woman like that waiting for me, I wouldn't make her wait too long."

Hunter was still trying to straighten his collar as he made his way to the Brenner House. The courthouse clock was striking six as he opened the door. He saw Nitika sitting alone in the middle of the dining room. She looked up when his boots hit the oak floor. The smile on her face was enough to wipe away the bad day he had. Nitika

51

stood when he approached her table and reached for the tie around his neck.

"Why is it that men can never get these things right," she said adjusting the tie.

"Sorry I'm late," he apologized. "That last wagon took longer to load than I hoped."

The waiter came over at that time. "I assume this is the young man you were waiting for. Are you ready to order now?"

"I'm not complaining, but why did you come out here? Is your father home now," he asked once the waiter left with their order.

"No. At least, not before I left."

"Then who's running the ranch? Don't tell me you left Doc in charge."

"I wouldn't do that to him," she said with a chuckle. "Allan sent Devon and Raven down to help out while I came to see you."

"What does Pinkerton have to do with this?"

"I went to see him about something," she said looking Hunter straight in the eye.

"Sweetheart, what's going on?"

"I went to find out if your father hired them to find you."

"Of course he would," he said defensively. "I haven't seen him in years. He wouldn't have known where I was living."

"The problem is, he didn't hire any detectives. But Colton Dagon did."

"Dagon? My father doesn't know him. What would he hire Pinkerton for?"

"According to William, to find a way to get you away from me. He told William that we were to get married and that you were getting in the way."

"What does that have to do with my father?"

Nitika took a deep breath. "That's what I came here to find out."

"Why did you go to Pinkerton in the first place?"

"When your father came to bring you home, he said the Pinkertons told him you were working for me. When I asked William, he said Colton hired him to find your father. It sounds to me like your father wasn't even looking for you. I'm beginning to wonder if your father is really sick."

Hunter took her hand. "You haven't seen him yet, have you?"

"Not since I got here, why?"

"He's not well, Sweetheart. He can barely work half a day anymore. He's lost weight and he's very pale. There's no doubt that something's wrong."

A woman approached their table. "There you are Brady," she exclaimed. "I went to your house, but your father said you hadn't come home yet. When I went to the docks, they said you had left to have dinner with a friend. Is *this* your friend?"

"Irena Braun, this is Nitika Brodie. Nitika owns the D Bar A Ranch in New Mexico."

"How nice," Irena said sweetly as she sat down uninvited. "It must be hard finding men who will work for a woman."

"Not as hard as it seems. Hunter didn't have a problem working for me."

"Who's Hunter," she asked, confused.

"That's the name Brady used when he worked for me."

Irena looked at Hunter. "Why would you ever want to change your name Brady dear?"

"You wouldn't understand," he said looking at his hands on the table.

"Well anyway, I was going to talk you into taking me to dinner," Irena said as their food arrived. "But I see you have already ordered. Perhaps another time then."

Irena flounced out of the room. She made enough of a commotion, that all the men couldn't help but watch her go. Everyone except Hunter. He kept his eyes on his plate, as he wondered what Nitika was going to think. Hunter had hoped the two would never meet.

Since he came back, Irena had been trying to get back together with him. She seemed to have forgotten why they broke up the first time. But he couldn't act like it never happened. It forced changes on his life he didn't want.

Although, in the end, it did bring him and Nitika together. But now, he was afraid Irena's sudden appearance tonight might end it. He was pushing his food around on his plate when Nitika took his hand. She wasn't the kind to jump to conclusions and he knew she would want answers first.

"No matter what, I still love you. What is Irena to you?"

Chapter 13

"She was my fiancé before I joined the army."

"What happened?"

"She tried to seduce me. When I refused, she got involved with another boy. She told her father that she was carrying my child. Galvin Connor threatened to have me thrown in jail if I didn't marry Irena. So my father made me join the army. She married Donald Braun shortly after that. He was killed in the war six months into his commission. She's been living off his money since. I have a feeling, she's about out of money."

"In other words, she's a gold digger."

"Yeah. I'm just glad I found out before I married her. She can be very difficult to deal with when she doesn't get what she wants. I knew I couldn't live like that."

"So you're saying I haven't been difficult to live with," she said with a crooked grin.

"Interesting, yes. Difficult, sometimes. But you, I'm too afraid of to do much about it."

The waiter cleared his throat as he approached their table. Nitika looked around and saw that the room was empty. She didn't know that it had gotten to be so late. Hunter paid for their meal as they left the room. The doors were closed behind them and the lights turned low. No one was at the main desk, leaving the lobby deserted.

Taking him by the hand, Nitika led Hunter upstairs. He looked up and down the hall before entering her room. Although he knew she didn't care, this was his hometown. Folks would still talk if he was seen entering a room with a young woman. Especially since some of them knew Irena had her eye on him.

The clock on the dresser woke Nitika first. She nudged Hunter until he mumbled something. He rolled over and nuzzled her neck. Throwing the covers off, she slid from under his arm. Nitika gathered up his clothes and dumped them on the bed.

"It's nine o'clock, Hunter."

He opened his eyes. "I was supposed to be at work an hour ago. My father's going to be livid when I get there."

"What's he going to do, fire you?"

"Funny. I wish it was that simple. Then I'd be able to come home with you. What are your plans for today," he asked reaching for his clothes.

"I'm going to check in with some former colleagues. See what I can get from them."

"You mean about the connection between Colton and my father?"

"Yeah. Raven told me the one to work on was Thomas Wilks."

"How do you know he'll tell you anything? I don't think he's allowed to talk to you about any of his cases."

"That's what Allan hired me for. He told me a pretty face could make any man spill all his secrets without him knowing it."

"I'm surprised you still worked for him. How many cases did you work on?"

"Probably about five or so. Mostly, I was with Devon and Raven. They usually get the more difficult cases to work. I was brought in when they would hit a dead end. Most men wouldn't think that a woman was a detective and would tell her anything."

"And you were okay with that?"

"I liked the challenge, and showing up Raven."

"Now that I can believe," he said donning his coat. "I want to take you to dinner tonight. There's a little restaurant down the street that I want to take you to. How about I meet you here around seven?"

"I'll be waiting for you."

Brady frowned at the clock as Hunter walked in the office. "You're late," he growled.

"I slept in," he mumbled.

"You didn't come home last night. Where were you?"

"I was with a friend."

"A lady friend," Brady asked expectantly.

"That's none of your business," Hunter said wondering at the sudden mood change.

"Do I know her," he asked chuckling.

"You've met," Hunter said tentatively knowing his father didn't approve of his relationship with Nitika.

"Don't let her keep you up late again," Brady said gruffly. "We've got too much work to do here for you to be coming in late every morning."

"Yes Sir," Hunter grated.

Nitika saw Irena sitting in the lobby when she came down. She wondered if the woman saw Hunter leave not more than ten minutes before her. As Nitika ignored her and headed for the dining room, Irena followed her. The woman sat down uninvited and glared at Nitika.

"I know Brady spent the night with you," she hissed.

"Were you lurking in the alley all night to find out," Nitika countered.

"I went to his house this morning. No one had seen him all night. I saw him leave a few minutes ago. Just what do you think you'll gain by that? Brady is my man."

"He *was* your man until he wised up and left you."

"We have a child together. Brady won't abandon us for someone like you," Irena said with disdain.

"That's not how I heard it," Nitika said picking up a menu.

"Well, think what you like. I plan on marrying Brady very soon," she said haughtily.

"Sorry to disappoint you, but we're already married."

Irena stared at her in disbelief. "Brady never said anything-." She stopped before she said too much.

Irena got up and left without saying anything more. Breakfast now forgotten, Nitika decided to follow her. She wanted to know which Brady she was talking about. From her reaction to the news, Nitika almost had the feeling that Irena was setting Hunter up for something. Nitika saw her hire a hack.

She looked up the street and saw another one sitting idle. The driver sat up when he saw the beautiful woman approach his rig. He jumped down and opened the door. Nitika took his hand as he helped her inside.

"And where would such a lovely lady be heading on this wonderful day," he asked sweetly.

"Cut the sugar talk," Nitika said settling in the seat. "I want you to follow that hack without being seen."

"No problem, Miss. Ain't nobody going to spot old Hansen," the driver said leaping aboard his rig.

They followed Irena as she drove past the docks. Her hack slowed but didn't stop as it passed by Brady Sr.'s office window. Hunter was nowhere to be seen. Irena went around the corner and into the alley beside the office. Nitika went a couple blocks further down and stopped.

"Ain't none of my business, Ma'am. But I hope you ain't planning something against the Huntingtons. They's mighty powerful folks around here."

"It's not them I'm after," Nitika said pulling out several bills. "Wait here."

Hansen looked at the money in his hand. "For this kind of money I'd wait forever."

Nitika made her way back to the Huntington Freighting Company just as Hunter left on some errand. She saw Brady draw the blind on his office and was able to pass by without being seen by the people inside. Irena's hack was still parked in the shadows of the alley. The driver was sitting on the seat as Nitika approached the alley.

Looking around the edge of the blind, Nitika could see Irena pacing back in forth in the office. Brady was seated behind his desk. The day was warm enough that Brady had his window open slightly, allowing Nitika to clearly hear everything they said.

"So my dear, how was your night with Junior?"

"What night? He wasn't with me last night."

"Oh? Then who was he with?"

"He was with his wife," she spat out.

"His what," Brady exclaimed half raising out of his chair.

"His wife. I met her yesterday at the Brenner House. I take it, you didn't know."

"Of course not," he bellowed. "Who is this woman anyway?"

"He said her name was Nitika Brodie. Brady said he used to work for her."

"Yeah, I know who she is," he growled.

"You promised me a quarter of this company if I seduced Brady into marrying me. How can I do that if he's already married?"

"Maybe she was just saying that to make you jealous. He didn't say anything when I went to bring him home. And those Pinkertons didn't mention it either. They don't usually miss things like that."

"Well, you better do something about it if you want Father to be your partner."

"I'll get to the bottom of it somehow," he said grudgingly. "You better go. Junior will be back soon and we can't let him see you here."

Nitika quickly left the corner of the building before Irena came out the side door. Hansen was still waiting for her when she got back. He helped her inside then vaulted to the seat again.

"Where are we off to now Miss?"

"Back to the Brenner House, Hansen. I haven't had breakfast yet."

"They done serving breakfast there now Ma'am. But I know this little place that makes the most delicious food you ever ate."

"Alright, lead on then," she said seeing Thomas Wilks walking down the street.

Chapter 14

Doc grumbled as he passed by the main house. Raven was lounging on the front porch with a glass of lemonade in his hand. In the time that he and Devon had been here, Raven barely did any work. Everyone knew he was only there to babysit the ranch while the bosses were away, but Doc expected him to do some work. His partner was up and ready to work before anyone else.

They all knew now that the fancy dude act was just that, an act. Devon could out work half the hands when he set his mind to it. He earned the respect of every man there after the first day. Several of the horses Doc was breaking knocked down the corral he was holding them in. While Doc and three others went in search of the stock, Devon took the rest to find logs to repair the corral. From what the men told him, Devon cut twice as many posts and planted most of them himself when they got back.

Devon came out of the house just as Doc entered the horse barn. "Bad day, Partner?"

"Yeah. Has been since Miss Nitika left," Raven said shifting in his seat.

"You shouldn't have carried her trunk down."

"I've carried heavier feed sacks," Raven commented.

"True, but that was before Hickory Jack's bullet messed up your knee. You ever going to tell Mr. Pinkerton?"

"I don't want to end up with a desk job."

"Raven, the doctor told you it'd only get worse. There'll come a time when you won't be able to move it at all. Then what will you do?"

"Don't know. But right now," he said painfully getting to his feet, "I need to find that liniment of hers. Colby needs some help tracking down some rustlers."

Doc came out dressed ready to break a few more mounts when he saw Raven in the office. He was looking through the drawers of Nitika's desk. Nodding to Dandy, he walked over to the house. The boy had no business in there.

"Just because you're pretending to be boss, that don't give you the right to look through her things," he snapped.

Raven ignored him as he continued to look for the liniment. "She told us to use her office if we needed to."

"Just what are you looking for anyhow?"

He opened a drawer and saw the jar, but picked up a notebook instead. "Just this."

Doc frowned and left. Raven dropped the notebook back down and got what he really was looking for. Two months of hiding the limp was starting to take its toll. The doctor said he wasn't able to find the bullet Hickory Jack hit him with. It was nearly a month before Raven could even put weight on his right leg. Now it seemed like the bullet shifted because the pain was in a different place.

Colby was waiting for him when he came out a few minutes later. He had two horses saddled and ready to go. Raven managed to mount without wincing. They rode out past the corrals as they headed for the east pastures. Doc watched them go before turning back to the bronc he was working with.

"What are they up to," Dandy asked.

"Don't know, but Raven seems to be influencing Colby. Ever since them Pinkertons got here, Colby ain't done a lick of work. They just ride off anywhere they please."

Devon came up and heard this last comment. "Colby and Raven are tracking a couple of rustlers that have been trying to get some of your cattle."

"Why weren't we told about it? We can stomp our own snakes," Doc protested.

"Because there are four new men since we were last here. We wanted to make sure they weren't part of the gang."

"You still could have told us," Doc complained.

"Nitika said you couldn't keep a secret. We didn't want to tip our hand if they were in on the rustling."

"Still the same ones," Raven asked Colby.

"Yeah," he said tracing the shoe print. "They're headed back to the old Oldrich place. Guess they figured they found a good hiding place. No one's lived in that house since I took the Oldriches to Texas."

"Anybody own the ranch now?"

"A syndicate out of Colorado bought it a couple months ago," Colby said swinging back on his mount. "But we haven't seen any activity over there since. You okay," he asked when he saw Raven rubbing his sore knee.

"Caught a bullet a couple months back. The doc couldn't find the bullet."

Colby only nodded, able to understand the kind of pain Raven must be in. He led out as they continued to follow the tracks. They could see smoke coming from the chimney of the main house as they came to the edge of the woods. Looking over at Raven, he saw the set of his jaw and knew Raven wasn't going to let his injury slow him down. Circling around to the south of the ranch house, Colby slipped up to the back porch. Finding a window that was shoulder high, he looked inside for the rustlers.

He could see the fire in the fireplace, but the men were nowhere in sight. Colby looked back to the woods, but only saw his horse. Raven had gone off to do some scouting, he assumed. Voices in the kitchen, made Colby duck out of sight behind some bushes. Soon, one of the men came out and headed for the outhouse.

Colby slipped from his cover and made his way to the other side of the house. He waited for the man to return before he began searching the house again. The men were lounging in the parlor. They hadn't even bothered to remove the dust covers from the furniture. Leaving the house, Colby made his way across the yard to the barn. He wanted to know exactly how many men they were facing. In the barn were three saddle horses and a pack horse. Colby wondered where the third man was at.

Raven didn't have to wonder where the third man was hiding. While Colby scouted out the house, he continued to circle the woods. It was hard for him to believe that there wasn't a sentry posted somewhere. The forest was thick around the ranch yard, creating a lot of places a man could hide. He was looking up into some of the thicker branches for possible ambush places when he was pulled from his horse.

His breath was knocked from him as he landed on his attacker. Raven broke free and rolled out of range of the ambusher's knife. The man quickly gained his feet as Raven struggled to stand. He closed in on Raven and took a swing at his stomach. Raven fell back to avoid the point of the knife aimed for his torso. His knee twisted as he fought to gain his feet again. The other man rushed him as he turned to face the ambusher.

Raven grabbed the man's knife arm and threw the man to the ground. He sprang to his feet and made another run at Raven. Again, Raven grasped the man's arm and wrenched the knife free. The man fought to get the knife back. He hooked his foot behind the man's leg and pulled them both down. Raven heard him gasp and felt blood running down his hand. Pushing his attacker off Raven saw the knife buried in the other man's chest.

Raven staggered to his feet, testing his sore leg. He grabbed his injured knee as pain shot up to his hip. His horse nosed his shoulder with concern. Leading him around, Raven managed to grab the stirrup. Pulling himself up, he kept his weight off his bad leg. Soon he was in the saddle and on his way to find Colby.

Chapter 15

Concerned when he didn't see Raven, Colby left the house and went in search of him. He was about to mount his horse when he heard a noise behind him. Drawing his gun, he ducked back into the brush. Raven emerged hunched over his saddle. Colby saw the blood on his shirt.

"You hit," he asked approaching Raven's horse.

"No. I found a sentry posted on the west side of the woods. How many more are there?"

"I saw three horses in the barn and two men in the house. We've got to get you back to the ranch," he said as Raven clutched his knee harder.

Colby gathered up the reins of Raven's horse. "What about the rustlers?"

"They'll keep for now. We'll have to get some of the men to come round up the fifty or so head I saw grazing behind the barn. We'll take care of the rustlers then. Right now, you need Doc's help."

Doc kept looking out toward the east. Colby and Raven had been gone almost the whole day. He only hoped that nothing happened to either of them, mostly Colby. But Nitika had a special place in her heart for Raven. That boy was going to get between her and Hunter unless he could get rid of him.

Nitika deserved a man better than that Pinkerton. Doc knew Raven was a good man, but he had a dangerous job. He didn't want Nitika to be left alone if anything happened to Raven. Dusk was coming on and there still wasn't any sign of the two men. He gave the brown mustang a slap on the rump and headed for the rails.

"What's going on Doc," Dandy asked as he followed his partner.

"Colby and Raven haven't come back yet. I'm going to go look for them."

He heard a horse snort as he dropped the rails to leave. Looking up, he saw Colby leading Raven's mount. The Pinkerton was slumped over the saddle, barely holding on. Colby headed for the main house. Devon came out as Colby dismounted.

"Where's Doc at," Colby asked tying the horses at the hitch rail.

"He's at the breaking corral." Devon saw Raven's face twisted with pain. "The knee, Partner?"

"Yeah," Raven groaned. "I think the bullet dislodged itself. Hurts something awful."

Devon helped Raven out of the saddle and half-carried him into the house. He saw Colby coming with Doc in tow, carrying his black bag. Once in the house, Devon took Raven to the guest room and laid him on the bed. Gently, he took Raven's boots and jeans off.

"It's really swollen, Pard. What happened out there?"

"The rustlers are hiding out at the old Oldrich ranch. Found a sentry patrolling the outskirts. Had to fight him," Raven explained fighting consciousness.

"Get hurt out there," Doc asked sarcastically.

Raven moaned before passing out. Doc saw the swollen knee and the blood on Raven's shirt and wondered what happened. The Pinkerton didn't seem to be hurt other than his knee, but he had to know the extent of all his injuries.

"Raven say anything about how he was hurt?"

"Two months ago, he took a bullet. The doctor couldn't remove it. Now he thinks it moved."

"Well that explains why he ain't done a lick of work since you got here. Let me take a look here," Doc said gingerly gripping Raven's leg.

"What the-," Raven groaned, jerking his leg out of Doc's hands.

"Easy Son. I just want to look at this leg of yours. Just let me know where it hurts."

Gently, Doc ran his fingers along the swollen flesh. Raven constantly flinched until Doc got close to the bullet. He touched a protruding area and Raven screamed. The bullet wasn't far from the surface, but it was lodged somewhere.

"I'm going to try and get the bullet out."

"Not if you have to take my leg," Raven said between clenched teeth.

"I'll do my best," Doc conceded. "That bullet has to come out. I can't promise you your leg."

With Devon keeping Raven sedated, Doc cut into the swollen knee near the bulge. He soon found the bullet, but was having trouble removing it. Even knocked out, Raven was still restless as Doc tried to work the bullet loose. Sweat covered his face as he finally pulled the bullet free. Doc bandaged the joint and splinted the leg.

"Is he going to be okay," Devon asked anxiously.

"He's young and strong. He should pull through just fine. How he survived this long like that, I don't know. He had to be in a great deal of pain."

"More than he would admit even to me," Devon said. "Will he lose his leg?"

"I saw worse wounds in the army than that. Long as no infection set in, although after two months I doubt it will happen now. He'll be just fine."

Raven woke with a mouth full of cotton and a throbbing head. He didn't recognize the ceiling. After a moment's thought, he remembered why he was here. Half afraid, he lifted the sheet and glanced down at his leg. A chuckle reached him from the darkened corner of the room.

"It's still there, Boy," Doc said with affection. "I had to splint it so it could heal right."

"Thanks, Old Man. Nitika's lucky to have you around."

"You'd best remember that when she comes back with Hunter," Doc warned.

Raven pulled himself up to look at the doctor. "I know what Nitika means to you. But she's a grown woman with her own mind. There's a time you need to let go."

"I'm the one who gave her life. I think I know more about what's best for her than you."

"She told me you were here when she was born. That still doesn't give you the right to tell her what to do."

Doc was silent for a few minutes. "I never told anyone this, but Nitika wasn't breathing when she was born. I was afraid she was dead and I couldn't let that happen to Dyami. I took Nitika to the other room and brought her back."

"Yeah well, I knew from the second day here, she already had her sights set on Hunter. Much as I didn't want to, I backed off. I found out a long time ago, she was a hard one to catch if she didn't want to be."

"Known her a long time, have you?"

"We worked a couple cases together. Couple times we pretended to be husband and wife. I thought there might be something there. Last time we were here, I thought perhaps we'd rekindle what we had. But Hunter was her man by the time we got here. I knew it was too late then."

"Yeah, then why did you keep after her?"

"Because I knew it bothered you something fierce," Raven said with a chuckle. "Colby go after those rustlers?"

"Yeah, caught them while they were getting drunk on some of Ethan's private stock that was left behind."

"I wonder what would happen if Nitika doesn't bring Hunter back. Would you object if I started courting her?"

"Get some rest," Doc grunted on his way out the door.

Chapter 16

Hunter was throwing a few things in his valise. The night he and Nitika spent together was the first real night of sleep he had gotten since coming home. He was hoping for the same thing tonight. Hunter saw his father was sitting in the study, a blanket draped over his legs, as he started to leave.

"Can I talk to you Son," Brady called out in a feeble voice.

"What is it Father? Are you feeling poorly?"

Brady shook his head. "Not any worse than any other time. No, I need to ask you something."

"What is it," Hunter asked impatiently looking at the grandfather clock in the hall.

"I heard that you were married. Is it true?"

"Who told you that?"

"Irena, if that really matters. I just want to know if you did marry that Brodie girl or not."

Knowing how his father felt about Nitika, Hunter knew the answer he wanted to hear. But with the news coming from Irena, it sounded like Nitika said it for a reason. Brady began drumming his fingers on the arm of the chair. Hunter was hesitating on his answer and Brady was beginning to think that there was no marriage.

"Yeah, we are," Hunter finally said setting his valise down.

"Why didn't you tell me? I never would have asked you to come home if I'd known. Why didn't her father say anything?"

"It was kind of sudden and we didn't have the time to tell anyone before you showed up."

Brady grunted. "You got her in trouble. Is that why you married her so suddenly? If you'd done right by Irena, none of this would have happened."

Hunter sighed. "I've told you many times, Irena and I never slept together. What ever child she may have isn't mine. I wasn't about to marry her because of another man's child."

"You still should have married her when you had the chance. Why did you break off the engagement anyhow?"

"Because she tried to worm her way into my bed long before she got involved with Tommy Roberts. After I broke it off, I found out that she'd been sleeping with several other men while we were engaged. How can you expect me to marry a woman like that?"

Hunter picked up his valise and stormed out of the house before his father could say anything more. If he didn't see for himself how his father had changed, he might believe Nitika was right. His father wasn't acting like a dying man. Nothing had changed around here, his father was just as difficult to live with now as he always had been.

So occupied with his thoughts, Hunter missed seeing the man hiding behind the tree at the corner of his father's property. Charles Dolby had been on his way to see Brady when he saw Hunter leaving. He was surprised to see the young man at home. From what Brady had told them, Hunter should have been at work. Once Hunter had disappeared around the corner, Charles quickly walked up the steps.

Brady frowned when he saw who was on the other side of the door. "My son see you?"

"I made sure he didn't. Besides from what I could see, he had his mind on other things."

"Most likely his wife," Brady growled. "Why didn't you tell me he was already married? I wouldn't have gone through all this if I'd known," he said indicating the ill fitting clothes.

"I assure you, I'm just as surprised as you are. When we located your son, he wasn't married. He was working on a ranch as the foreman."

"Yeah well, he married the boss lady just before I got there."

"You mean he married my client's intended? Perhaps I'll just have to look into this. It sounds a little fishy to me."

Mary Beth Huntington entered the study after Dolby left. "What do you have to say for yourself now, Brady?"

"Don't start with me woman," he growled.

"I told you to leave Brady alone. He never wanted to take over the business. I knew this was a mistake."

"He's ruined all my plans," he mumbled.

"What do you plan to do now? You can't keep him here forever. He has a family to go home to."

"He has family here," he shouted. After a moments thought he said, "I'll come up with something."

Nitika had been following Thomas Wilks all morning without his knowledge. She had an idea as to how to meet him. Spending her time shopping while keeping an eye on him, Nitika had amassed a large quantity of packages. When she saw him coming down the boardwalk, she stepped out in his path. Too late to stop himself, Thomas ran right into her. Exaggerating her fall, Nitika let her purchases land where they may.

"I am so sorry, Ma'am," he blurted, reaching for the closest parcel. "Let me help you with these."

Nitika righted her hat and dusted off her skirt front. "Thank you Sir. How clumsy of me." She stood and began picking up the smaller boxes. "I really should have had these sent to my hotel."

"At least let me help you take them to your room," he insisted.

"That isn't necessary. I can handle them myself," she said struggling to balance them all.

"There's too many here for you. Let me take these big ones," he pleaded.

Nitika conceded and led the way to her hotel. Thomas was more focused on watching her than where he was walking. Several times, he nearly dropped his load. Getting him to talk was going to be easier than she thought.

Hunter knew Nitika wasn't going to be in her hotel room when he tied his horse outside. The desk clerk saw him enter. As he started up the stairs, the clerk stopped him.

"Your lady friend isn't up there right now."

Hunter nodded and continued up to her room. Using his knife, he managed to pry open the door. He dropped his bag on the floor by the bed. His lunch break was almost over and he needed to get back to the office. Looking forward to tonight, he opened the door and looked down the hall. He heard Nitika's voice as he shut the door behind him.

Nitika saw him as she topped the stairs. She dropped a package and he heard a man's voice behind her. Using this distraction, he ducked back into her room and hid in the wardrobe. He heard Nitika and some man enter with packages rattling.

"Just set them down on the bed," she said, seeing the valise on the floor.

"Have you eaten yet," he asked piling her boxes on the bed.

"No, I've been so busy shopping. I completely forgot about eating."

"Why don't I take you out to lunch?"

"Oh no, I couldn't let you do that. You've done enough just by helping me up here. I couldn't let you buy me lunch."

"Please, I hate to eat alone. Besides, it's not everyday a man gets to eat with such a beautiful lady, Miss Braden."

"Call me Angela," Nitika said sweetly.

"Then you must call me Thomas. Shall we go?"

"If you insist," she said as they left.

Chuckling as he emerged from the wardrobe, Hunter straightened up Nitika's clothes. He saw her gun belt hanging beside the taffeta dresses and shook his head in wonder. She really could be anyone she wanted. From what he heard, Nitika was very good at "working a skirt". Secretly, he was hoping she would find out his father was faking his illness. He wasn't this kind of a business man and he wanted to go back to the ranch with her.

But until he knew for sure, he was going to have to keep working at the freighting company. As he went to leave, he saw Nitika's room key sitting on the bed. Picking it up, he locked the door behind him. The clerk was still at the desk when he came down.

"Your lady friend is a busy woman, Mr. Huntington. She just left with Thomas Wilks. He's a Pinkerton, you know."

"I know all about it," Hunter said waving him off.

Chapter 17

Riding his horse back to the office, Hunter went past the little café where Nitika and Thomas were eating. Though she looked completely enamored with whatever tale he was spinning, Hunter knew she saw him ride by. He grinned once he was past them. Nitika certainly was playing up to the Pinkerton. It was no wonder Allan used her when it took a lady's touch.

Hunter saw the man standing on the dock before he got there. From his stance, Hunter knew Robert Connor was angry. He hadn't seen Irena's brother since he moved back home. Taking his time, Hunter put up his horse in the stable. Let the man wait, Hunter thought as he threw his saddle over the rail. He heard a noise behind him.

"Heard you were married, Huntington," Robert said entering the stable.

"What of it," Hunter said leaving the stall.

"Irena's pretty upset about that," he answered. "She had her heart set on marrying you. How could you go and marry some tramp?"

"I could say the same thing about her," Hunter said as he walked past.

Robert grabbed his arm and turned him around. "What do you mean by that?"

"Irena isn't exactly as innocent as you think," he said jerking loose from Robert's grasp.

Hunter could see the punch coming, but wasn't fast enough to dodge it. Robert's fist hit him square on the cheek. He was staggered by the blow, but kept his feet. With a roar, Robert charged at him. Hunter sidestepped him, punching him in the head as he rushed past. Robert hit the floor with a thud.

Lumbering to his feet, Robert shook away the cobwebs. His eyes roamed the stable until they found Hunter. Bringing his hands up in front of him, Robert advanced again. Hunter backed out into the open. He knew that Robert was the best pugilist in his college class and he wanted room to work.

Robert threw an uppercut that Hunter easily blocked, but it left him open to the quick jabs to the ribs. Hunter threw a few of his own punches, but only encountered air. Connor grinned as he took advantage of Hunter's lack of skill and landed a few good punches to his midsection again.

Feigning a right cross, Hunter managed to slip inside Robert's defenses and land a hard punch to the face. Robert's head snapped back with the impact. He took a couple steps back, but didn't fall. Rubbing his jaw, Robert circled warily until he shook off the punch. Hunter had more power behind his fists than he first thought. He had to end this fight soon. Robert couldn't lose face now.

Hunter's style showed signs of barroom brawling. Robert decided to lower himself to Hunter's level. He rushed at Hunter with his arms outstretched. His arms wrapped around Hunter and propelled them out the large front door of the stable.

Hunter gasped as Robert landed on top, knocking his breath out of him. Robert began to squeeze his arms around Hunter's middle. He became aware of people around them as Hunter began to black out. Soon, Robert released him and stood up. Still on the ground, Hunter sucked in great draughts of air.

"This ain't over Huntington," Connor warned as he stalked off.

"Mr. Huntington," Harvis Johns said coming to Hunter's side as he shakily got to his feet. "Are you okay?"

"I'm fine Johns," Hunter said brushing off the office clerk's hand.

"Maybe I should send for the doctor," he said nervously.

"No, I don't need him," Hunter said touching his side. "Just get back to work. All of you."

Hunter went into his office and sat down. He gingerly touched his cheek. Without seeing it, he knew there was a bruise forming. His ribs hurt, but they didn't feel broken. Nitika would see the bruise and ask him about it. Desperately, he wanted to go to her and ask her why she said they were married. It did feel good to know that she wanted to be married to him. First things first, though. His father's illness, real or not, had to be handled.

Thomas Wilks was droning on about some of the cases he'd worked over the years. Nitika was feigning interest, hoping he would mention Brady Huntington. Raven was right. It didn't take much to get him to talk. She saw Brady ride past in a carriage and watched him for awhile. Thomas saw her eyes looking out the window. He saw who she was watching.

"That's Brady Huntington. He owns the Huntington Freighting Company."

"He doesn't look like he'll own it much longer. He looks very ill."

"That's just makeup," Wilks said.

"Really? What would a man like him need to look sick for?"

"He wants his son to take over the business. But he's not on good terms with him."

"Then why try and make him take over? I mean if the son doesn't want to be here, why make him?"

"Well, it's complicated," Thomas said looking into his coffee cup.

"How so," Nitika asked leaning closer.

"I really shouldn't be talking about this. It's still a case under investigation."

Nitika let the subject drop. She didn't want to make Thomas suspicious. He continued to talk about his adventures, trying to impress her. Soon, they were the only ones in the restaurant. Nitika suggested they walk around town. Thomas pointed out different sights along the way. They walked past Huntington's and Nitika saw Hunter bent over paperwork in the office.

Won't be long now, she thought. Even though she couldn't see his face, she knew how unhappy he was cooped up in the stuffy office. They stopped and watched one of the wagons being loaded. The springs complained as the last crate was heaped on top and the whole thing was tied down.

Nitika convinced Thomas to take her back to her hotel. She was getting tired of his company and she didn't think he'd tell her anything more. A woman seemed to be waiting for someone in the lobby when she entered. When she bid Thomas goodbye, the woman came over to her.

"Nitika Brodie, I assume," she said.

"Can I help you," Nitika asked, warily.

"My name is Mary Beth Huntington, Brady's mother. I wanted to meet his wife, without his father around."

Nitika looked at her "mother in law" across the table from her. Mary Beth was very much the opposite of her husband. She was very warm and friendly. It almost made Nitika feel guilty about lying to her, almost. But if she would let it slip and Brady found out, the whole ruse would be for naught.

"I told Brady it was a mistake to try and make Brady come home. My oldest son never did like being indoors. I think that's why his father was always so hard on him. Brady just doesn't understand."

"I could tell Hunter, I mean Brady, wasn't happy when I came to town. If his father wasn't sick, he wouldn't have come back."

Mary Beth was silent for awhile. "What are you willing to do to get Brady back?"

"Whatever it takes. Why?"

"My husband isn't sick. But Brady won't believe us. We'll have to get proof that my son will believe."

Chapter 18

Colton Dagon hadn't heard anything more from William Pinkerton since learning that Hunter had gone home. He thought a couple weeks was enough time for Nitika to realize she needed a man to run things for her. The sheriff wasn't happy when he saw Colton renting a buggy. Nodding to the man, Colton rode out of town.

As he crossed onto D Bar A land, he began planning what he would do with it all. Sure he'd keep part of it for raising cattle. But he didn't particularly care for animals. He had heard rumors that there was an oil deposit on her land somewhere. Another reason for marrying her. He had to get his hands on that oil. There was no telling how much money it would bring in.

Raven frowned when he saw the buggy driving up. He didn't know who the man was, but he looked like some kind of dandy. No man that Nitika would be interested in. The man pulled up in front of the house. Several hands showed up as he looped the reins over the hitching rail. They didn't look very friendly toward this stranger.

"I am looking for the lady of the house," the man said in the way of an introduction. "Is she at home?"

"Who might you be," Raven asked sitting up to get a better look at him.

"My name is Colton Dagon. I happen to be Miss Nitika's intended. And who might you be?"

"Raven Keary. And I'm ramrodding this outfit. What is it you want with Miss Brodie?"

"I came here as soon as I heard she had lost her foreman. I thought perhaps she needed my help. Is she here?"

"She's gone off to bring her man back," Doc growled approaching Colton. "And if you don't clear off of here now, we'll help you leave again."

Colton looked offended as he took a step back. "Are you going to let him talk to me like that," he whined, looking at Raven.

"Seems to me like he's in his rights, seeing how Miss Brodie ain't here to do the honors," Raven commented.

"Just what kind of foreman are you to allow the hired help to insult guests?"

"I didn't say I was the foreman. I'm just here holding down the fort until Miss Brodie comes back from Georgia."

Colton paled at the news that Nitika had gone to where Hunter was. He was certain she would find out the whole thing was a hoax. What he didn't know, was that she knew he was behind everything before she even left. Devon rode up and saw the man surrounded by the hands.

"What's going on here," he demanded.

"Man claims to be Nitika's fiancé. Though Doc says different."

"I thought Hunter was her man," Devon said. "Well, Doc does know more than the rest of us. We'll just let him handle this one."

"That's right Mr. Pinkerton Man. I told you we stomp our own snakes," Doc said cracking his knuckles.

"You work for Mr. Pinkerton," Colton stuttered.

"That's right," Raven said resting his hand on the gun in his lap. "We both do. So does Nitika, once in awhile."

Dagon swallowed hard. He didn't think that Nitika was anything but a fancy skirt. Knowing that she was a detective, albeit part time, made him realize she was capable of finding out his plans. Colton had to get to Savannah fast. Everything depended on it.

"It appears I've made a long trip for nothing," he said, sounding dejected. "I was hoping that Nitika had changed her mind about that foreman of hers. The man is no good for her."

Colton climbed back on board the buggy and turned it around. He forced himself to ride slowly out of the yard. Once out of sight of the house, he urged the horse to a trot. He had to get back to the station to catch the first train east. All of his dreams were dashed in that one brief conversation.

Seeing he had a three hour wait for the next train, he sent off a telegram to the Pinkerton agents in Savannah. His train was scheduled to arrive in the middle of the night, giving him the cover of darkness in which to slip into town. He couldn't let Nitika see him at all and he was in need of a place to stay. The more he knew about her whereabouts, the easier it would be for him to avoid her.

Dagon went to the café next door to think. Once he got to Georgia, he needed to find an ally. Not having the freedom to move around like he wanted, someone had to tell him what was going on. He didn't know that he could rely on Brady Huntington. Whatever deal William made with him, Colton didn't know. But that only made the man an unknown factor. Brady was just as ambitious as he was and would do anything to get what he wanted.

Perhaps he could get a woman to help. Brady Jr. wasn't a bad looking man. Surely there were women willing to play dirty in order to get their claws in him. These were all things he was going to have to find out from the Pinkerton detectives. He was even willing to give them a cut in the ranch once he acquired it.

Sheriff Donnish walked in the café and sat down across from him. "Didn't think you'd ever come back here Dagon. Thought Miss Brodie told you to get out of town."

"I'm headed East tonight, if you need to know Sheriff," he said.

"Saw you go out to the D Bar A Ranch earlier. Surprised you came back in one piece."

"Since when did my welfare become your business?"

"The minute you stepped off the train you became my business. And you will be until you leave."

"Don't worry Sheriff. I won't be here much longer." For now, he thought.

Donnish grunted and left the café. He didn't trust that man. Nitika didn't point guns at just anyone. Being sheriff, he was able to ask questions other people couldn't. A few telegrams got him everything he needed to know about the lawyer. And what he found out, he didn't like.

Colton was known for going after rich women. He had been engaged to at least four other women with the kind of money that Miss Brodie was sure to have. Three of the engagements were broken off by the women. The last one, he broke off. Donnish assumed it was so he could pursue Miss Brodie. It happened about the time Nitika inherited her father's half of the ranch. That was the main reason he was lounging across the street from the café. Someone had to keep an eye on the snake.

Dagon was fuming in his coffee after the sheriff left. That man was sticking his nose where it didn't belong. Nitika wasn't going to get away from him. And no two bit sheriff was going to get in his way. Brady Huntington Jr. was going to be enough of a problem for him to get rid of. He knew that Brady could out fight him with fists or guns. But he wasn't a match for Colton's brain.

Top of his class, no one was even close academically. It didn't take much thought to draw a gun or throw a punch. No, Brady wasn't a match for him. He heard the train whistle as he left the café with his luggage. Soon, he thought, Nitika would be his.

Chapter 19

Nitika left Mary Beth and headed back to her hotel. Two blocks later, a carriage pulled up beside her. Brady Huntington stuck his head out. She ignored him as she continued to walk. Her hand gripped her reticule tighter, feeling the weight of her gun in it.

"Get in," he growled.

"I don't think so Mr. Huntington," she said still walking.

The carriage stopped and the door swung open, blocking her way. "I said get in," he said.

Nitika stepped in, brushing aside his hand. The driver whistled to the horse as she settled in the seat across from him. As the carriage clattered along, Nitika took in the sight of Brady Huntington. The loose fitting clothes were a nice touch to add to his illness act. A frown on his face accented the "sunken" cheeks.

"Junior told me the two of you are married," he growled.

"That's right. What about it?"

"You carrying his child?"

"No. And even if I was, we're both adults. What we do is none of your business."

"What would it take for you to walk away from him?"

"Nothing you could ever offer would make me leave Hunter," she said definitely.

"Everyone has a price my dear. The only question is, what is your price?"

"What is it you have against me?"

"My son is too good for you. He deserves better than you."

Nitika crossed her arms across her chest. "Really. And Irena is more his type? Is that what you're telling me?"

"She is in the same class as Junior. You are not."

"You're right. I'm not in her class. If I was, I'd have a few men on the side to provide for me when Hunter wasn't around."

Brady pointed his finger at her. "I will not have you bad mouthing a woman of Irena's status like that. Now, how much is it going to cost me to get rid of you?"

"You want a price," she asked.

Brady nodded, reaching in his coat pocket for the bank draft he carried. This was easier than he thought. The girl was ready to deal with him. She had a price after all.

"Your son's freedom," she said as he began to withdraw his hand.

"I beg your pardon," he said caught off guard.

"You want to get rid of me. Release Hunter from his obligation to you."

"You don't understand. I'm willing to offer you whatever money you want to walk away."

"Don't insult me by offering me money, Mr. Huntington. You can't possibly believe that I am hard pressed enough to take money from you."

Brady frowned at the woman across from him. Nitika saw her hotel and knocked on the door. The driver stopped the carriage and she opened the door. As she stepped out, Brady grabbed her arm.

"You're making a mistake, Missy. You need to think about my offer."

Nitika pulled free from his iron grip. "I've already given you my answer."

She hurried into the hotel before he could come after her. The desk clerk saw her standing by the front door. Once Brady disappeared around the corner, Nitika hurried next door to the telegraph office. Nitika needed Raven and Devon's help to make her "marriage" real. Brady might try to check it out and she wanted something there for him to find.

"Mr. Huntington, Sir," Harvis said trepidly. "Are you sure you don't want me to get the doctor?"

Hunter's eyes shot open and he lifted his head from his desk. "What time is it?"

"It's five o'clock, Sir. All the wagons are gone for the day."

"I think I'm going to quit early tonight. Close up for me Harvis."

"Yes, Sir. You going to the doctor's?"

"No Harvis. I'm going to go get some sleep. This," he said touching his tender side, "is nothing I haven't handled before."

He rode his horse around behind the hotel. Wincing as he dismounted, he put up his mount in one of the stalls. After taking care of the animal, he went around front and walked into the lobby. The desk clerk saw him and opened his mouth. Hunter glared at the man and he quickly closed his mouth.

"Do you have nothing better to do than spy on your guests," he growled.

"Yes Sir, I mean, no Sir. I didn't mean to sound like a busy body Mr. Huntington," he stammered.

Hunter stalked up the stairs to Nitika's room. He tried the door and knew Nitika hadn't come back yet. Taking the key from his pocket, he let himself in. Her packages were still on the bed and his valise was where he left it. From the shape of some, Hunter could tell what was in them. There were several hat and other garment boxes. Along with perhaps a couple shoe boxes. He was beginning to wonder which was the real Nitika. His Nitika didn't need all these clothes.

Carefully setting them all on the floor, he stretched out his long frame on the bed. Tilting his hat over his eyes, he was able to block out most of the light. It was nearly suppertime and Nitika should be back soon. He planned to take a short nap before going out to eat.

It took Nitika longer than she thought to compose her telegram. She had to word it so that Raven could decipher it but Brady couldn't. The telegraph operator looked at the strange message before sending it. He shook his head, but kept his mouth shut. Used to sending out cryptic messages for the Pinkertons, he just sent what he was given without wondering why.

Now back in her hotel, Nitika made a play of looking for her key. "I must have left my key up in my room," she said to the clerk. "Can you let me in my room?"

"Of course," he said smoothly, grabbing the ring of keys from the wall behind him. "You've had a rather busy day today, haven't you?"

"What do you mean by that?"

"From all the packages I saw you bring in and the gentlemen who have been keeping you company, it's enough to keep any lady busy."

"Anyone ever tell you sticking your nose where it doesn't belong is a sure way to get it cut off," she asked him coldly as he turned the key in the lock.

"I seem to be having that kind of problem today, Ma'am. Anything else I can do for you?"

"Not right now," she said seeing a pair of boots on her bed through the crack in the door.

Nitika watched the clerk hustle back down the stairs before going in her room. Just as she thought, Hunter was asleep on the bed, fully dressed. At least he put my things on the floor first, she thought as she took his boots off. She gasped in surprise when she lifted his hat and saw the bruise on his cheek.

Hanging the hat on the bedpost, Nitika went back downstairs. "Does the hotel have an ice house?"

"Yes Ma'am. Did you need some?"

She nodded. "I need a little bowl of ice pieces."

The clerk wanted to ask why, but thought better of it. He had already angered Brady Huntington as well as her and he didn't want to get into more trouble. Quickly he went outside to the small shack beside the livery. A few minutes later, he handed her the ice. He watched as she headed back to her room.

Taking her handkerchief, Nitika filled it with ice and placed it on Hunter's cheek. The sudden coldness woke him with a moan. He opened his good eye to stare at her. Nitika took his hand and placed it on the ice pack.

"Hold that in place. It'll help with the swelling. So, who's virtue were you defending this time," she asked with amusement.

"Mine, Wife," he growled.

Chapter 20

Nitika saw something change in his stare. "Sounded good, didn't it?"

"Yeah," he said reluctantly, "it did. Why did you tell Irena we were married?"

"She made me mad," Nitika said working on the top button of his shirt.

Hunter chuckled. "I never took you for the jealous type. What'd she say to you?"

"That she was going to marry you and that you wouldn't abandon her and your son."

"Terrence isn't my son," he declared stilling her hands.

"I know. You told me," she said freeing her hands to continue unbuttoning his shirt.

"Honey, I'm too tired tonight," he protested grabbing her hands again.

"Is that all men think about? You've been in a fight. I want to see how bad the damage is. Doc did teach me a few things about patching up the men after a night in town. What happened anyhow?"

"Irena's brother paid me a visit. He wasn't happy that I upset his sister," he said resigning himself to her administrations.

"And he did all this because Irena is upset with you," she asked looking at the bruises on his torso.

"Well, I kind of said some things he didn't like to hear about her."

Nitika gently ran her hands along his ribs. He tensed when she found sore spots, but nothing felt broken. Laying there Hunter remembered what she said about Doc.

"Just what did Doc teach you about doctoring on men?"

"He taught me how to tell if something's broken and how to sew up cuts. I was too young to do much more except hand him things he needed."

"Just how many men did you see naked?"

"Now who's the jealous one," she joshed. "I wasn't allowed in the room if someone had their pants off."

"What did you find out from Mr. Wilks today?"

"Not a lot. He caught himself starting to say too much and quit talking. I didn't push him any. With that clerk downstairs knowing you're up here, he might find out my real name and I definitely won't get anything from him then."

"I was hoping to take you out to eat, but I don't feel up to it right now."

"Nothing's broken, but you will be sore for a few days," she said. "Do you want me to see if they'll bring something up for us to eat?"

"Don't worry about that. You're with a Huntington. This town will do anything for you."

Nitika heard the bitterness in his voice. It's no wonder he changed his name. She went down to the dining room to order their meals. The cook was more than willing to fix anything he had in the kitchen regardless of whether it was on the menu or not. Ordering two of the specials, she headed back to her room. Hunter had some of her boxes on the bed, looking through them. He was holding up a filmy nightgown, a devilish grin on his face.

"I figured you'd find that one."

"So when do you want to make this marriage official," he asked putting the nightgown back in its box.

"When we get back home. If we do it here, your father will find out and know we lied."

Hunter set the boxes on the floor again. "That maybe a long time to wait 'Tika. I don't know how long it will take to settle things here."

"I saw your father today," she said joining him on the bed.

"I told you he was a sick man."

"He offered me money to leave you."

"I can't believe he did that. I mean, I know he's capable of doing something like that. I just didn't think he would. And to you of all people. He must really be sick."

"I got an up close look at him. What I saw was make-up, not illness. Sweetheart, he's not dying."

"How can you be sure it's make-up? What about the weight loss?"

Nitika went to her trunk and pulled out a small box. She brought it back to Hunter and opened it. Taking a brush and powder, she carefully covered the bruise on his cheek. Then she handed him a mirror. Hunter couldn't believe what he saw, or rather what he didn't see.

"How'd you do that," he asked still looking at himself in the mirror.

"I used some disguises when I worked for Allan. Devon is a master at it. He taught me a thing or two. I know a make-up job when I see one. Whoever does your father's is quite good. As for the weight loss, your father probably just bought bigger suits."

"I just can't believe he would go through all this to help a man he never met. Something has to be wrong."

Nitika let the matter drop. She knew arguing would only push Hunter away and that was the last thing she wanted to do. Besides, she and Mary Beth had a plan in place to catch Brady in the act. A maid knocked on her door, a tray in her hands.

"Just leave it outside the door when you're done, Ma'am, I'll pick it up in a little while."

The maid passed a handsomely dressed man on her way back down the stairs. He stopped and watched her descend and go to the dining room. She looked back and giggled as she disappeared. Thomas Wilks continued up the stairs. While there wasn't an Angela Braden listed as a guest, Nitika Brodie was the one staying in the room he took the packages to.

From what his partner had told him, Miss Brodie had claimed to be married to Brady Huntington Jr. He was on his way to her room to find out for sure. Still kicking himself for going on like he did, he probably cost him and his partner a great deal of money. The D Bar A Ranch was one of the largest in New Mexico. And they would have gotten enough to retire on. But how could she have known he was a Pinkerton? They had only met that morning.

"Do you think the men will listen to Devon? He doesn't strike me as the working type."

"Allan said he used to be a foreman before joining the agency."

"What about Raven? Was he ever a cowboy before becoming a detective?"

"He drifted a lot, so he could have. I know he used to break horses."

Hunter was silent for a moment. "When you worked with them, did you ever," he asked not willing to finish his thought.

"I pretended to be Raven's wife before. And while he was willing to go all the way with the ruse, I wasn't. When they came to help the last time, Raven thought he could get somewhere with me because of it. I think that's why Doc hates him so much. He thought Raven would get between us."

"You and I both know that wouldn't happen."

Wilks backed away from the door. He had heard enough. Any chance they had of retiring early were gone. They might not have a job once Allan knew what they did to one of his own detectives. He had worked with Raven and Devon and knew how protective they were of their friends. And from the sound of things, Nitika Brodie Huntington was a very good friend. Thomas was deep in thought and didn't see the couple coming up the stairs. He accidentally bumped into the man. The man's bag landed with a thud and he began to protest.

Hearing the commotion, Nitika went to the door and looked out. She saw Wilks handing the man his bag back. She went back to pick up the empty tray. Setting it outside, she returned to Hunter's side.

"Looks like my cover's blown now. Wilks was just here. I'm guessing he was listening to us talk."

Chapter 21

Hunter was at the office early the next morning. Finally rested, he was ready to take on whatever the day brought. It didn't hurt that Nitika would be waiting for him when he came back. She had worn her new nightgown and he saw the bruise on her arm. When he asked her about it, she was reluctant to tell him. He still couldn't believe his father was strong enough to bruise anything. But Nitika had no reason to lie about it either. Hearing skirts swishing, he looked up expecting Nitika.

"Mother," he exclaimed. "What are you doing here?"

"Can't a mother drop by to see her son at work? Besides, I haven't seen much of you lately. I figured this was the only way to spend some time with you."

"I've been busy," he mumbled.

"Yes, I know. With your wife. When do I get to meet her? Why haven't you brought her to the house?"

"Father doesn't like her. I didn't want to cause trouble for Nitika by bringing her home."

"That's an unusual name," Mary Beth said sitting down. "How did she get such a name?"

"It means Angel in Kiowa. Her father is half blooded."

"She's an Indian," she asked pretending surprise.

"Is there something wrong with that?"

"Not at all Son. I just didn't expect it. No wonder your father hates her."

"Why does he hate her?"

"I don't know for sure. But I know he hates all Indians. Now, when do I get to meet the woman who stole your heart?"

"She's meeting me here for lunch in about an hour. You can join us if you like," he said hoping she had plans.

"Then I guess you won't mind me waiting here for her then, do you?"

"Not at all," he said, forcing a smile. He had hoped to have Nitika to himself.

Nitika was surprised when she walked into his office. She had excepted him to be alone. Mary Beth noticed the change to his face when he saw Nitika. This woman was definitely the one for her son. His love for her was unmistakable.

"From my son's reaction, I take it you're Nitika," she said standing up.

"Yes I am. Hunter?"

"Sorry," he said straightening up his desk. "This is my mother, Mary Beth Huntington. Mother, this is Nitika."

"So, I finally get to meet the woman who stole my son. And I say it's about time someone did. I was beginning to think I'd never become a grandmother."

"Mother," Hunter blurted. "It's a bit early to be thinking about children."

"Nonsense. I'm sure Nitika's parents are thinking the same thing."

Nitika looked at Hunter, hoping for an escape. Seeing none, she said, "My father doesn't know about us yet. We didn't have time to tell him before Hunter, I mean Brady, left."

"What about your mother Dear? Oh I'm sorry, I didn't think that she might not be living."

"She's alive and well, Mrs. Huntington. She's living in Virginia. Mother thinks Father was killed two years ago. She's moved on with her life with a new man. We don't always see things the same way. The last place she wants to be is out at my ranch."

Hunter rubbed his eye then winced. He had forgotten about the bruise. His hand came away with powder on it. Nitika had put make-up on it this morning before he left. Mary Beth saw it and gasped. She took Hunter's chin in her hand to look closer at the bruise.

"What happened Son?"

"Robert Connor paid me a little visit yesterday. He wasn't happy that we were married."

"So he hit you? Because you married someone other than his sister?"

"Mostly," Hunter said ducking his face.

"Let me guess, you made him angry," Mary Beth said accusingly.

"I couldn't let him get away with bad mouthing Nitika," Hunter protested standing up. "Shall we go to lunch now?"

Colton saw Nitika on the arm of Hunter as they entered a restaurant. He assumed the stately looking woman on his other side was his mother. Hiding in the carriage, he watched the trio sit down at a window table. Somehow, he had to get Nitika away from him. It was time he paid the Pinkertons a visit.

Dolby was just leaving the office when Colton's carriage stopped in front. "Are you Wilks or Dolby," he asked the man.

"Who wants to know," Dolby asked, his hand reaching in his coat for his gun.

"Colton Dagon. Which one are you?"

"Dolby. What can I do for you Mr. Dagon?"

"You can get in, for starters." Once they were riding down the street, Colton told him what he wanted. "My fiancé is still seeing Brady Huntington. I just saw the two of them together. Our plan isn't working. We need to do something else."

"What do you have in mind?"

"Is there a woman who wants Brady bad enough to work with us?"

Dolby smiled. "Irena Braun. She was once engaged to Brady. She wants him back. Mrs. Braun is devious enough to do anything."

"Do you know where I can find her?"

"Not off hand, but she shouldn't be too hard to find."

"I can't be seen around town. Nitika will see me. I'm staying at the Winston Hotel. Bring Mrs. Braun to me."

Colton left him at the front door of Irena's house. While she wasn't home, the maid knew where she was going. After a little footwork, Charles was able to find her in the dress shop. Being there many times with his wife, he wasn't uncomfortable wandering among the wares. Irena was getting fitted for a new ball gown.

"I have a proposal for you my dear."

Irena looked at the detective. "You can't afford me," she said cooly.

"I don't mean me. How far will you go to get Brady back?"

"As far as it takes. Why? What do you have in mind?"

"It's not me, it's my client. He wants his fiancé back."

"It's a little too late for that," she said bitterly. "They're already married."

"We don't believe it's real."

"Then why would they lie like that?"

"Maybe Miss Brodie was just saying that to keep you away. Have you asked Brady?"

"His father did. Brady didn't deny it. In fact, he's moved in with her at the hotel. I don't see him doing that if they weren't married."

"We're checking into this. In the meantime, there's a Colton Dagon staying at the Winston who wants to talk to you. If this marriage is a fake, you could still get Brady back."

Curious, Irena met with Colton. While she detested the man, she did like what he had to say. He wasn't happy when she told him Brady and Nitika were married. But he didn't believe it was real either. They figured if she could somehow coax Brady into bed where Nitika could find them together, Nitika would leave him.

Colton's plan was to be there to pick up the pieces of her broken heart. Irena would convince Brady that it was her that he loved and not Nitika. In exchange for each other's help, they were going to share the profits from both businesses for a year. With all the partnerships he formed to try to get Nitika, he was going to need something to replace all those lost profits.

Chapter 22

Devon and Raven went into town to send a wire to Allan about their assignment. Raven was going to make sure Devon didn't tell their boss about his knee injury. The telegraph operator handed them a yellow envelope while Devon wrote out the wire.

"Got that yesterday afternoon. I was going to bring it out today once Walt could come to watch the key."

"What's it say Partner," Devon asked without looking up.

"It's from Nitika," he mumbled scanning the contents.

"Well, what she want?"

"I'll tell you later," Raven said stuffing the telegram in his pocket.

After Devon sent his wire, the detectives went next door to the café for coffee. "Out with it Raven. What's Nitika want us to do?"

"I think she's wanting us to fake some documents," Raven answered pulling out the wire again.

"Yeah, what kind," Devon asked warily.

"You tell me. Listen to this: Found what I wanted Stop. Looks like Kansas again Stop. Need some help to prove it exists Stop. Tell Devon he's doing a good job on the ranch Stop. Check tally on line eight in ledger against Red Nose's harem Stop."

"Kansas is where you two were 'married', right?"

"Yeah. Kind of wished it was for real," Raven said with a smile.

"She must have told people she's married to Hunter. And she needs you to fake a marriage certificate in case someone comes looking."

"I'll need one to copy. You think there might be one in the house?"

"Maybe, but it might not be from here. Alexander never married and I don't know where Nitika's folks were married exactly."

"This has to be done now, so we best start looking for one."

Doc saw Raven rummaging through Nitika's office and growled. "Just what do you think you're doing now? This is still Miss Nitika's office."

"Where was Dyami married," Raven asked refusing to argue with the man.

"Here at the ranch, why?"

"Do you know if their marriage certificate is here somewhere?"

"What do you need Mr. Brodie's license for," he groused.

"Just tell me where it's kept," Raven said getting angry.

"Nitika keeps all her important papers in the safe in the floor. If it's here in the house, that's where it would be. Good luck figuring out the combination."

Raven lifted the rug and found the floor safe. He pulled out the telegram again. Nitika gave him a clue to the combination in her message. In the bottom of her desk drawer were three ledger books. Knowing that Red Nose was one of her bulls, he looked at line eight in all three. Only one book mentioned the ornery beast, but there was only two sets of numbers. Then he realized that eight was the third number of the combination.

Quickly spinning the knob, Raven soon had the safe open and was looking at her papers. Doc came back to the office and saw he had the safe open. The ranch hand sauntered in and sat on the edge of the desk.

"Safe cracker too, huh? Nitika ought to be glad I'm here to keep an eye on you."

"Nitika gave me the combination to the safe. She told me to do this. Now if you don't mind, I have a job to do."

Doc picked up the telegram and read it. "I don't see nothing here saying to tear her office apart. And what's this about Kansas?"

"She was my wife then. Wished it was for real, though. She really is something special."

"Yeah. You just better remember that too when she comes home."

Raven was silent while he continued to go through the documents. Doc realized then just how much Raven was in love with Nitika. He was willing to lose her to another man if it made her happy. Maybe that was what was bothering Doc about him so much. He had seen the predatory look in the detective's eyes every time he saw Nitika and he didn't like it. But at least he was man enough to back off when the lady wasn't interested.

The slam of the safe door shutting brought Doc out of his daze. Raven had the document he wanted in his hands. A wishful look crossed his face as he read over Dyami's marriage license. Shaking himself of thoughts left alone, Raven went in search of his partner. Doc followed, still wondering what they were up to.

Devon was in the kitchen with a small case open in front of him. In it he had an assortment of inks and pens. He looked the license over before selecting a sheaf of paper that was similar to it. Doc watched as he meticulously copied every detail of the document. Beside him was a copy of Nitika's signature as well as one from Hunter. The detective then copied Nitika's handwriting to perfection.

"Just what is this all about," Doc demanded.

"When did Hunter's father show up here," Devon asked instead.

"About the seventh, why?"

"Do you know the exact day he came," Raven asked. "It's real important that we get the day right."

Doc thought about it some more. These men were up to something, but Nitika was asking them to do this. "Yeah, it was the seventh. Now what is this all about?"

"What name do you think Hunter used," Devon asked, pen poised above the line.

"He's been calling himself Hunter Tilton. Nitika didn't know any other name until Brady showed up at her door," Raven said looking out the back door.

Devon nodded and scribbled down Hunter's name. He wrote Taos County in a blank and some illegible name at the bottom. Holding up his artwork, Devon looked the paper over. Doc came closer and read the certificate. Raven looked out the back window again and saw an empty yard. Whoever had been leaning against the awning post was gone.

"Just what are you faking a marriage license for?"

"Nitika told some people she was married to Hunter. She wants this around in case someone comes investigating. She's dealing with some very rich and powerful people in Savannah and she wouldn't put it past them to stoop this low," Devon explained.

"Why didn't you say that in the first place instead of making me wonder?"

"Because someone was listening in back there," Raven said jerking his thumb over his shoulder.

"Yeah," Doc said going to the window to look out. "Who was it?"

"One of the new hands. He might have just been taking a break, but we weren't taking any chances."

"Now what," Doc asked.

"We just see what happens," Devon shrugged.

Chapter 23

Mary Beth was startled when she saw her husband's carriage going down the street. "What is he up to?"

"Who Mother," Hunter asked following her gaze.

"Your father. His carriage just went by with him in it. Looks like he's headed for the theater district. What would he be doing down there at this time of day?"

Hunter looked at Nitika, but saw only a blank expression. He knew what she was thinking, though. Because he was having the same thoughts. Maybe he was just wanting to believe her, but Hunter had an urge to follow his father to see where he went.

Quickly paying their bill, Hunter went to flag down a hack. Nitika nodded to the one across the street. The driver pulled over to their side of the street and Hunter looked at Nitika. She only smiled as they entered the cabin.

"Where to Ma'am," Hansen asked leaning over to her side.

"Do you know what Mr. Huntington's coach looks like?"

"Every driver in town knows what it looks like," he said with a toothy grin. "You want me to find it for you," he asked seeing who the other passengers were.

"It went toward the theater district, Hansen. Just don't get caught looking for it."

"Looks like you've made some useful friends Nitika," Hunter said as they got rolling.

"They come in handy, for a price."

After checking out three buildings, Hansen found the coach behind a little theater house that didn't even have a name out front. Hunter jumped out and headed for the back door. Nitika was fast on his heels. She grabbed his arm before he opened the door.

"Don't go in there half-cocked."

Hunter jerked his arm free. "You can't stop me from finding out what's going on."

"I'm not. But if you go in there like this, you'll spook whoever is helping your father."

He took a deep breath. "What do you suggest we do?"

"Quietly check all the rooms until we find your father. The coach is still here. I don't think he'd park it here and go to another building."

Mary Beth joined them as they opened the back door. They each looked in a room and continued down the hall until Mary Beth came to one that was locked. Hunter placed his ear to the door and thought he heard his father. Stepping back, he kicked the door in. A woman screamed as Brady fell off the bed with a thud.

Hunter couldn't believe what he saw. The woman tried covering up with the sheet while Brady frantically searched for his pants. Mary Beth saw them on the other side of the bed and retrieved them. She dangled them over his head.

"Looking for these," she said, an icy tone in her voice.

Brady reached for them, but Mary Beth threw them out in the hall. He came to his feet with a roar only to get slapped across the face. Stunned, he stared at his wife while he rubbed his stinging cheek. He sat down on the bed before he saw Nitika.

"What are you doing here?"

"I'm just along for the ride. Hunter is the one who wanted to follow you."

"Only because you poisoned his mind against me."

Hunter had been staring at his father's appearance. The sunken features of his face were smeared. Nitika had been right, his father was wearing makeup to look sick. Without clothes, his body didn't look like he had lost any weight.

"You're not sick, are you," he asked his father.

"Of course not Junior," he snapped.

"Why pretend?"

"Because I was offered a partnership in a ranch if I could keep you here long enough."

"I'm guessing the ranch is mine," Nitika said.

"Yeah," he growled. "Dolby and Wilks are involved too."

"Sounds to me like Colton is spreading my money a bit thin."

"What are you talking about," Hunter asked her.

"Colton offered William Pinkerton ten percent of my ranch if he could get rid of you. Now, if he offered Dolby, Wilks and your father the same amount, then he only gets sixty percent. That wouldn't be enough to make him happy."

"You knew all this, didn't you Nitika?"

"I know a lot more than that, Hunter. Your father was trying to get you and Irena married so her father would sell his business to him. Irena was going to get a quarter of the business here as well."

"Why didn't you tell me," he asked despondently.

"Would you have believed me before this?"

Hunter sank down to a chair, his head in his hands. "I don't know what to think."

Nitika knelt in front of him. "I didn't want to tell you anything until I had proof. I knew how it would hurt you and I wanted to make sure I was right first."

"I've gotta get out of here," he said standing up.

Nitika sat still as Hunter left the room. Brady had managed to crawl out to the hall to drag his pants back in the room. The woman was still hiding in her bed. Mary Beth blocked his escape. He stood to put them on, heedless of Nitika's presence.

"What do you have to say for yourself Brady?"

"This is none of your concern woman," he grumbled as he finished dressing.

"You are my husband. This *is* my concern. I hope you have a cot at the warehouse because you aren't getting back in the house."

"I own the house," he hollered. "You can't keep me out."

"Watch me," she hissed. "Let's go Nitika."

Nitika followed Mary Beth out of the theater and back to their hack. Hansen was twirling his quirt around his finger when the ladies got to him. He quickly jumped down and helped them inside. Mary Beth seemed composed as they rode back to town. What they had found at the theater wasn't what Nitika had expected.

"I always suspected Brady of being unfaithful," Mary Beth finally said. "I just didn't want to believe he actually would."

"What are you going to do now?"

"I don't know. I can't leave him. I don't have any way to support myself."

"There's plenty of room at my ranch, if you want to live in the middle of nowhere. We could build a small cottage for you."

"Thanks for the offer, but I don't want to intrude. You and Brady haven't been able to spend much time together since you got married. I'm sure you want to be alone."

"I need to tell you something. We're not really married. I told Irena that to make her mad."

"I see. Do you plan on getting married?"

"Yeah, as soon as Hunter asks me. That is, if he still wants to marry me after this."

"You're good for him Dear. He'll ask you. Even if I have to stand over him while he does it."

They got back to the hotel, but there was no sign of Hunter. They began searching town for him. Hansen willingly drove them all over town in search of him. Mary Beth remained inside the hack while Nitika looked inside the various saloons they came to. She finally spotted Hunter standing at the bar of the Red Slipper Saloon. There was already an empty bottle in front of him and he was working on a second one.

"Is he in there," Mary Beth asked once Nitika rejoined her inside.

She nodded. "It looks like he's working on getting completely drunk. He's already on his second bottle."

"Come stay with me at the house Nitika. I'd enjoy the company."

The bartender took the empty bottles away from Hunter with a shake of his head. He had been surprised when Brady Huntington Jr. stalked into his bar and demanded a bottle. The elder Huntington only patronized the high class saloons. Yet his son was drinking with the common man. Then again, Brady Jr. had been gone for seven years. There was no telling what kind of life he'd lived.

"Give me another," Hunter demanded.

He was weaving on his feet and his words were badly slurred. The bartender shook his head. Brady was too drunk to stand, let alone drink anymore. "Sorry Mr. Huntington, but you've had your limit here. Why don't you go get yourself some sleep?"

Hunter glared at the man through blood-shot eyes. When the bartender stood his ground, Hunter staggered out of the saloon. He saw a woman crossing the street toward him. It looked like Nitika and she was waiting for him to leave the saloon. The woman, wearing a hooded cape, came up to him and he leaned against her.

Irena turned her face away from his whiskey laden breath as she guided Hunter back to the hotel. This was going better than she had hoped. After her talk with Colton Dagon, she had an idea as to how to get Nitika to leave Brady. Marriage or no marriage, she and Colton were determined to break them up.

No one was at the desk when the couple made their way up the stairs. Irena searched Hunter the best she could as he leaned against her for support. Finally finding the key, she opened the door and helped Hunter to the bed. Hunter collapsed on the bed with a sigh. Irena began to undress him.

"What would I do without you Nitika," he slurred as he closed his eyes.

Chapter 24

Mary Beth was serving Nitika tea when they heard a commotion at the front door. Brady was trying to get in past the barricade they had set up. As they reached the entryway, the side window began to open and Brady's head appeared. Instinctively, Nitika pulled her gun out of the pocket of her skirt. Seeing the black bore aimed at his head, Brady ducked back out. He went around to the door and began to bang on it.

"You can't keep me out of my own house," he bellowed.

Soon lights started coming on around the street. Dogs barked at the disturbance, bringing townsfolk out of their homes. Unaware of the attention he was getting, Brady paced across the porch. He tried the windows and the door time and again. Returning to the door, he repeated his tirade.

"This is my house and I demand that you let me in," he yelled.

"Why don't you go back to your actress," Mary Beth shouted back.

After ten minutes of trying to get in, Brady saw a policeman walking his way. "Officer, I need your help. I locked myself out of my house and my wife won't let me back in."

"Yeah, I know. Your neighbors told me all about it," he said knocking on the door. "Mrs. Huntington, are you alright in there?"

"We're fine," she said through the door.

"We? Who else is in there with you?"

The officer heard a heavy object being moved before Mary Beth appeared in the doorway. "My daughter in law is here with me."

"Why won't you let Mr. Huntington in the house?"

"Ask him," she said bitterly as Nitika joined her at the door.

"Arrest her," Brady said pointing at the younger woman. "She pulled a gun on me."

"Ma'am, did you aim a gun at Mr. Huntington?"

"Of course."

"Why," the policeman asked surprised by the candid admission.

"He was trying to get in through a window. I thought he was an intruder. I was only protecting us."

Brady glared at her. "Stop the innocent act. You knew it was me you were pointing that cannon at."

"Exactly what kind of gun are you carrying," the officer asked jokingly.

His face fell when he saw the .44 in her hand. He had expected a derringer or some other small gun. The young woman seemed more than capable of using the gun she held. But why would someone of her obvious sophistication need such a large weapon?

"May I ask why you have a .44 Smith and Wesson?"

"It's come in handy working for Allan Pinkerton as well as on my ranch," Nitika answered putting her gun back in her pocket.

"You're a Pinkerton agent," the officer Dancy asked doubtfully.

"I have been on a few occasions. My badge is in my hotel room if you'd like to see it."

"You can't seriously believe she's a detective," Brady blurted out. "This is just some tale to get you to believe their side of the story."

"Mr. Huntington, your neighbors are complaining about you disturbing the peace. They are the ones who sent for me to arrest you. And unless you settle down, I will be forced to do just that."

"This is my house and I will do whatever I want. I don't care what my neighbors think."

Tired of his tirade, Officer Dancy slapped the handcuffs on Brady. The man had a lot of fight in him for being as sick as he was supposed to be. He was stronger than Dancy thought he should be. Perhaps the women needed to come along as well.

"Can I ask you ladies to follow me to the jailhouse? I would like to ask you some questions. And Mrs. Huntington, would you be so kind as to retrieve your badge for me. I'd like to verify your identity."

"Of course. The Brenner House is along the way. I'll be there as soon as possible."

Mary Beth had the stable hand hook up the buggy for them while she changed into a more comfortable outfit. She had a feeling that they would be there for quite awhile. She was just as surprised to find out that Nitika was a detective. That would explain why she knew as much as she did about what Brady was planning.

"How long have you known Brady was faking his illness?"

Nitika looked out into the darkness outside the buggy. "I had a feeling something wasn't right when he came to get Hunter. The way he was acting didn't sit right with me. He told me that the Pinkertons had told him where to find Hunter. All I did was ask Allan who really hired him. The whole thing came out then. But I knew Hunter wouldn't believe anything I said unless I could show him solid proof."

"What else do you know about Brady's dealings?"

"I know he offered Irena a quarter of his company if she married Hunter. And that her father would sell out to him if they married. From what I understand, Brady would be a very rich man if that happened. Plus he'd get a piece of my ranch in the bargain."

"What a man won't do for money," Mary Beth sighed. "I'm just glad Brady, I mean, Hunter isn't like his father. He doesn't crave wealth like Brady."

The buggy stopped in front of the hotel and the driver helped Nitika down. A different night clerk was at the desk and smiled as she walked past. Working the late shift he hadn't gotten a look at the woman married to the most sought after bachelor in Savannah before. Seeing her now, he knew Brady Huntington Jr. was a very lucky man.

Nitika opened her door and heard snoring. Hunter had somehow made it back and was passed out on the bed. Figuring he was still dressed, she turned up the lamp by the bed. She was surprised to see a dark head resting on Hunter's chest. The woman stirred when the light hit her. She picked her head up and blinked awake. Irena smiled when she saw who was there.

"Looks like Brady prefers me to you after all," she said smugly.

"Actually," Nitika said, grabbing hold of the sheet, "it looks more like you crawled into bed with a drunk."

Nitika whipped the sheet off the bed. Irena yelped in surprised as she tried to cover herself up with her hands. The cold air and Irena's cry startled Hunter awake, and he promptly fell out of bed. He sat there a moment trying to figure out how he ended up on the floor naked. The wood bit into his tender flesh as he looked around him.

On the bed was a naked Irena and standing over him was a fully dressed Nitika. Somehow he thought it should have been Nitika in the bed with him. After all she had been the one who brought him home, hadn't she? All this thinking was too much for his whiskey laced brain to comprehend and he decided to go back to sleep.

"How dare you," Irena hissed at Nitika once she go over the shock.

"How dare I," Nitika echoed. "You're the one in bed with my husband, drunk as he is. You've got one minute to get out of my room before I throw you out."

"You can't do that," Irena spat out as she climbed off the bed.

"Watch me," Nitika said gathering up the woman's clothes.

"What are you doing," Irena said in a panic as Nitika walked to the door.

"I'm helping you out," she replied imitating Mary Beth by throwing the garments out into the hall.

Furious, Irena rushed at Nitika, her fingers curled like claws. She stopped short when Nitika drew her gun. Even in her enraged state,

Irena noticed how calm Nitika was. Irena could sense the deadliness behind the cool exterior. Nitika wouldn't hesitate to shoot.

"Get out, now," Nitika said calmly though she felt anything but.

Hissing like a scalded cat, Irena stalked out into the hall and gathered up her pile of clothes. A door down the hall opened and she rushed for it, holding her things in front of her. She pushed past the dumbfounded gambler and slammed the door in his face. Seeing the other woman holding the gun, he knew better than to stand in the line of fire. This cat fight was too dangerous for his taste and he hurried down the stairs.

Nitika put her gun away and went over to Hunter, still sleeping on the floor. She threw the sheet over him before pulling out her makeup case. From the false bottom, she withdrew her badge and commission papers from Allan. Hunter mumbled in his sleep as she walked to the door. Locking it behind her, she went to rejoin Mary Beth.

"What's wrong Dear," Mary Beth asked when she saw the disquieted look on Nitika's face.

"I just caught Irena in bed with Hunter," she answered leaning back against the seat.

"Like father like son, I suppose. I'm sorry Honey."

"I don't think it's like that. Irena conned her way into bed with him, I'm sure. Hunter's beyond sauced. He probably doesn't even know how she got there."

"How do you know he's drunk?"

"Because Hunter doesn't snore when he sober."

Chapter 25

Nitika was resting her head on the table she sat at. The policemen all had to look over her identification, because none of them had ever seen a woman detective. Dancy sent a wire to Chicago for verification, but Nitika knew it wouldn't come back until early morning. Allan wasn't about to be disturbed at three in the morning.

Three times, she and Mary Beth had to repeat their story as to why Brady Huntington was cooling his heels in their jail cell. The first two times, the officers had thought it was amusing. Once Wilks had been dragged from his bed and brought down, they began to get serious. Now, Thomas sat across from her watching her try to sleep.

"Is he really worth all this?"

Nitika picked up her head and rubbed her eyes. "I almost lost him once. I won't do it again. So yeah, he's worth all this."

"I never would have taken you for a Pink. If I hadn't overheard you talking, I probably still wouldn't believe it."

"Why do you think I'm so good at my job?"

"You really married to him? I mean, no one seems to know for sure."

"There's another Pinkerton on my ranch, isn't there?"

111

Wilks grinned. "You are good. William had him planted there when Colton Dagon first approached him about splitting you two up."

"Trying to find out how much money he'd make, right? Well once I leave here, Jackson better be off my land. My men don't take kindly to spies. I mean, they almost killed Devon the first time he stepped onto my ranch. If I hadn't identified him, there's no telling what they would have done to him."

"Yeah, if they find out about him, his life's not going to be worth much."

Wilks was allowed to leave once Dancy came back from escorting Mary Beth home. She had refused to leave Nitika at first. But Brady went into a rage every time he caught a glimpse of her through the bars of his cell. He set a cup of coffee down in front of Nitika.

"I'm sorry about keeping you like this, but if we find out you're lying, it'd be easier to arrest you here."

"You're only doing your job. Besides, you're keeping me from what I really want to be doing anyhow," she said with a tired grin.

Dancy waited for her to elaborate, but she just drank her coffee. Not wanting to pry, he went to check if there was an answer to his telegram. It finally came through at six o'clock and he let Nitika leave. He shook his head as she wearily climbed into a waiting hack. What some women didn't do for the man they loved.

"Where to Ma'am?"

"The hotel, Hansen. I need to pick up a few things then over to the Huntington estate."

Hunter was sitting in the hotel dining room, his hands wrapped around a cup of coffee. The acrid taste of his cigarette added misery to the hangover he was suffering from and he put it out. When he woke this morning, he wondered why he was on the floor. After a few minutes of pondering, last night came back with a rush. He didn't know how he ever could have thought that Irena was Nitika. Although, he had never been that drunk before.

His stomach roiled at the smell of the other patrons' breakfasts. Nitika had to be furious with him. What happened when she found him in bed with Irena, he didn't know. Nor did he know what happened after he passed out. Nitika hadn't spent the night in the room, of that he knew for sure. Somehow he had to find her and make things right with her.

"Good morning Mrs. Huntington." He heard the clerk say.

Hunter bolted for the stairs. Nitika came down a few minutes later with a bag in her hands. He could see the dark circles under her eyes. She hadn't slept much last night, wherever that was. Standing at the foot of the stairs, Hunter blocked her path. He had do whatever it took to make her listen.

"I know you're mad at me," he began. "But I didn't know it was Irena last night. I thought it was you."

He saw her shoulder drop and braced himself for the slap he thought was coming. Nitika caught him off guard when her fist came in contact with his face. The blow knocked him to the floor, blood flowing from his broken nose. Hunter laid there, his hand covering his face.

"I deserved that," he said trying to staunch the blood. "You have every right to be mad at me for what I did. But I promise, I had no idea she was there."

"Irena conned her way into your bed," she said tiredly. "That wasn't your fault."

"Then why did you hit me," he asked tilting his head back.

"Because you got so blind drunk, you didn't know who you were sleeping with," she said stepping off the bottom step.

Her skirts bushed over his face as she walked past his prone form on the floor and out the front door. He was still laying there when the clerk came over to him. The man began fussing over him despite his protests.

"Let's get you to the office while I go for the doctor," he said helping Hunter up.

Nitika was sucking on her knuckles when she approached Hansen's hack. The driver didn't say a word as he helped her inside. He saw the reddened knuckles when she stretched her hand toward him. The lady had hit someone pretty hard. And he knew that only one person could make her that mad.

"Husband do something stupid," he asked shutting the door.

"You could say that. Just take me to the Huntington estate, please."

Hunter was guided into the manager's office to a settee. The clerk hustled out of the room in search of the doctor while he laid down. Gingerly, he touched his nose and knew it was broken. He thought Nitika had lied about using her bag when she broke Raven's nose. She had plenty of power behind her fist alone.

She wasn't mad at him like he thought. Nitika was smart enough to recognize Irena's devious plan. But she was mad that he fell for it. So shocked by her outburst, he never even asked where she was last night. Once his head stopped pounding, he was going to find her. The doctor came in and began fretting over him.

"Your nose is broken Son. Matthews said it was your wife that hit you. Is that true?"

"I didn't need you to tell me it was broke," Hunter growled at the grinning doctor.

"No need to get in a huff," the doctor said. "I only meant that you really must have done something terrible for her to hit you that hard."

"You have no idea," he said, closing his eyes against the pain.

Hansen twisted around and glanced down inside his coach. Mrs. Huntington was curled up on the seat sleeping. He had waited outside the jailhouse all night for her. What they wanted with her that long, he didn't know. But she didn't appear upset when she left. When he got to the Huntington mansion, he debated about waking her up. She managed to rouse herself when he opened the door.

Mary Beth met her at the door. "I have a room ready for you. I'm sure you'll want to get some sleep." She saw the reddened knuckles. "Can I assume my son was the cause," she asked picking up Nitika's hand.

"Who else could have made me that mad?"

Chapter 26

Irena was sitting in her carriage outside the hotel that Colton Dagon was staying at. The longer she waited for him, the madder she got. Their plan to break up Nitika and Brady backfired on them. She was the one who was humiliated when Nitika threw her clothes out into the hall. Next time, Colton was the one who would try something, she wasn't going through that again.

Colton finally came out and she had her driver stop him. The man looked confused when he looked in the darkened coach. With some urging from her driver, Colton entered the carriage. He was forced into his seat when the driver took off.

"How did your night with Brady go, my dear," he asked straightening his hat on his head.

"It didn't," she spat out.

"What happened," he asked peering at her in the shadows.

"I found Brady coming out of one of the saloons. I managed to get him back to Nitika's hotel room. The fool was so drunk, he passed out before I could do anything."

"What did you do then," Colton asked wondering what went wrong.

"I got into bed with him. Sooner or later, Nitika was bound to come back. I wanted her to catch us together."

"I take it she never came back," he said, watching her agitation grow.

"She came back alright," Irena ground out. "She threw my clothes out into the hall. I had to get them then find some place to get dressed. I have never been so humiliated in all my life."

"Couldn't you have just gone back into her room?"

"She put me out by gun point," Irena cried. "I didn't have a choice."

"Did she throw Brady out as well?"

"No, she just left to go who knows where. Brady was still on the floor as far as I know."

"Well, that still doesn't mean she didn't get rid of him later. You have to find out for sure."

"Forget it," she fumed. "I can't show my face around here right now. This time it's up to you. See if you can do any better."

"Nitika is not at all like I thought she should be. Perhaps it's going to take force instead of trying to out think her," Colton mumbled more to himself than to Irena. "I'll have to give this some thought. I am sorry things didn't work out for you, but things might not all be lost just yet. I will be in touch."

Brady Huntington was pacing the jail cell he was being kept in. How dare the police arrest him on his own front porch. Without him, most of them wouldn't even have their jobs. He couldn't believe they would take the word of a couple of women over him. The fact that one of them was an Indian made him seethe. And to top it off, Nitika claimed to be a Pinkerton agent. It made him laugh to think that the police actually believed her. The cell room door swung open and he saw a man coming in.

"Morning Mr. Huntington," Dolby said closing the door behind him. "I was surprised to hear you were in here. What happened?"

"My wife thinks she can tell me what I can do," he said. "She locked me out of the house. The neighbors called the police on me and I ended up here. Don't they know who I am?"

"Everyone knows who you are Mr. Huntington."

"Why are you here," Brady growled.

"I have some news you might find interesting."

"Will it get me out of here?"

Dolby smiled. "My partner's working on that right now. He enjoys playing a lawyer."

"Yeah, well he weren't doing that last night. He was here keeping that woman my son married company."

"That's what I came to talk to you about. Your son isn't married."

"How do you know," Brady asked coming up to the bars.

"We had a man planted on her ranch right after Colton Dagon got William Pinkerton to help find you. He overheard Devon and Raven falsifying a marriage certificate for your son and Miss Brodie."

"Who're Devon and Raven," he demanded.

"They are a couple Pinkertons that know Miss Brodie. From what our man told us, they're there to watch over things while Miss Brodie came here to expose you."

"She's done a good job of that," he conceded. "She caught me with the actress that was doing my make-up job. My wife was with her as well as my son. That's when Mary Beth threw me out. When I tried to get back in, that woman pulled a gun on me."

"Your wife tried to kill you," he asked incredulously.

"No, Miss Brodie tried. She claims she's a Pinkerton. You know anything about that?"

"I don't, but I'll ask Thomas."

Just then, Thomas walked into the room followed by a deputy. "The charges against you have been dropped Mr. Huntington. You're free to go."

"What were you doing here last night with that woman," Brady asked Thomas.

"Identifying her for the police."

"Is she really a detective?"

117

Thomas looked at his partner before nodding. "I did a little checking on her this morning. According to Allan himself, she's one of the best agents he's ever put in the field. And the way she managed to pull one over on me, I'm inclined to agree with him."

"No woman is that good. She had to have help."

"Nitika Brodie isn't your typical woman."

"When did she figure out that I wasn't sick," Brady asked once they were outside the jailhouse.

"According to Allan's notes, when you showed up at her ranch. The way you treated people made her think you weren't dying. She left for Allan's office right after you left with your son. Nitika is not one to act on a whim. Mr. Pinkerton sent her old friends to the ranch so she could come here. From what I accidentally told her, she figured everything out. I have a feeling she was waiting until she could catch you in the act before she went to your son with her evidence.

"Her entire plan was to get Brady to see that you weren't sick without him leaving her. She wasn't about to lose him like that. Miss Brodie is really in love with your son."

"They ain't getting married if I have anything to say about it. I won't have that woman spoil my family with her tainted blood."

The Pinkertons looked at one another but didn't say anything. They both knew about Brady Huntington's hatred for Indians. Brady and his sister were orphans in Colorado when a band of Indians found them hiding in a cave. His sister was taken in by one family while he went with another. Soon his sister fell in love with one of the young men. They married not long after that.

When a troop of soldiers found the small band of Indians, they were able to free Brady from them, but his sister refused to leave her new husband. The lieutenant in charge forcefully removed her from the tribe. She escaped sometime in the night and returned to them. When Brady went to get her to come back, she sent him away.

This made Brady angry and he vowed never to get involved with Indians again. His sister would be living in luxury with him if she had just left the Indians. Instead she's most likely still roaming from place to place trying to outrun the army.

Chapter 27

Hunter left the hotel office to look for Nitika. He saw the man who had been driving her around. The driver frowned when he approached the hack. Whether it was for personal or monetary reasons, the man didn't like him. Like him or not, Hunter still needed to find Nitika.

"Your wife do that," Hansen asked pointing at his face.

"Yeah, she's got quite a punch," Hunter replied, gingerly touching his face.

"I don't know what you did, but good for her," Hansen nodded.

"I did something stupid and I need to find her and explain. Do you know where she is?"

"Yes I do, but I'm not telling you. That's something you'll have to find out yourself. The lady obviously doesn't want to see you."

Hunter didn't know where she might have gone. Though he should have gone to the office, he went to his parents' house instead. Mary Beth answered the door and was shocked to see Hunter's face. Nitika hadn't told her how the fight ended.

"What happened Son," she asked reaching for his face.

"Nitika and I had a fight," he explained following her into the study.

"Looks like she won it. Both your eyes are black," Mary Beth said gently touching the smudges around his eyes.

"She's got quite a punch," he said sinking down into his father's chair. "Where's Father at anyhow?"

"He's in jail," she said matter of factly.

"What," Hunter exclaimed sitting upright. "What happened?"

"I kicked him out of the house. When he tried to get in, the neighbors called on the police. He was arrested for disturbing the peace."

Hunter couldn't believe what she said. He was surprised that the police would arrest his father in the first place. Brady Huntington was one of the most powerful men in town. He was above the law, or so Hunter always thought. Sinking back into the cushions, Hunter leaned his head back.

"I've lost her Mother," he moaned.

"Nonsense Dear," she chided. "Nitika loves you. She'll get over it."

Hunter shook his head. "I don't think so. I can't blame her, though. After finding Father with another woman, she catches me with Irena. I wouldn't be surprised if she never speaks to me again."

"She wouldn't have married you if she didn't love you enough to forgive you."

"We're not married Mother. Nitika said we were to make Irena jealous. She'll never marry me now, even if I asked her."

"You'll never know unless you try," she said seeing Nitika standing in the doorway behind Hunter. "I'll be back Son."

Mary Beth left the room and patted Nitika on the shoulder. She motioned for her to stay put. Nitika watched Hunter rub his forehead. That punch she hit him with must have given him a headache. Feeling guilty, she almost went in to him, almost. But Mary Beth returned carrying a small box.

"Are you alright Son?"

"My head is still buzzing from getting laid out flat by Nitika. How could I have ever thought Irena was her? They are nothing alike."

"You love her, don't you?"

"More than anything, Mother. She's my whole life. I never thought it could happen. She found a way under my skin like no other woman ever could."

"Then ask her to marry you," she said placing the box in his hand.

"What's this," he asked opening the box.

"It's your grandmother's ring. I want you to have it."

"I don't know. What if she turns me down?"

"You'll never know unless you ask me," Nitika said coming up behind him.

Hunter turned to face her. Nitika winced when she saw the bruises on his face. It made her feel even guiltier to know she was the cause of them. He was still holding the box with the ring. Swallowing hard, Hunter extended that hand.

"Despite everything that's happened, are you still willing to marry me?"

Nitika approached him and covered the ring with her hand. "What do you think?"

She kissed him gently on the lips, mindful of his broken nose. He flinched when he saw her arm move. Only this time she punched him in the shoulder. Hunter resisted the urge to rub the sore spot.

"If you ever do something that stupid again, I'll break more than your nose."

"Yes Ma'am," he said with a crooked grin. He pulled her down into his lap. "Where were you last night?"

"I was at the jailhouse," she said settling against his shoulder.

"All night?"

"The police thought it was amusing that I said I was a Pinkerton. They had to telegraph Allan to know for sure. I had to stay there until Allan answered them this morning."

"What for," he asked nuzzling her neck.

"So that I was easy to arrest if I was lying to them, or so they said."

"I should get to the office," he said.

"Harvis is taking care of the office today, Son," Mary Beth said. "You should just go get some rest."

"Is Harvis capable of running the office?"

"He ran it when your father came to bring you home. I'm sure he can handle it for one day."

Hunter was silent for awhile. "Did you know Father was faking his illness?"

"Yes I did Son, but don't be angry with me. It was a mother's selfishness. I wanted to see my son again. And I thought that if it was the only way to see you, then I wouldn't say anything to you about it."

"Am I the only one who doesn't know what's going on in my own family? How could you do that to me Mother?"

"Son when you left for the army, you vowed you would never step foot in this house again. That was the worse thing a mother could hear. I was willing to lie to you if it meant seeing you. Any mother would have done the same."

Nitika snuggled closer as Hunter tried to stand up. He realized she had fallen asleep in his lap. Not wanting to disturb her now, he settled back in the chair. Mary Beth retrieved a blanket from the closet and draped it over the two of them. The past day finally caught up with Hunter and he was soon sleeping as well.

Someone knocked on the door as she walked past it on her way to the kitchen. When Mary Beth opened the door, Brady barged his way in. She was knocked to the floor as he slammed the door shut. Crab-walking backwards, she tried to stay away from the enraged man in front of her.

"I'll teach you to lock me out of my own house," he sneered as he followed her.

Mary Beth reached the study doorway and turned a fearful eye to the sleeping couple. Brady saw where her gaze went. He saw Nitika sleeping in the arms of his son. Crazed with fury, he unleashed an animalistic roar.

"What is she doing in my house!"

Chapter 28

Startled awake Hunter jumped to his feet, effectively dumping Nitika on the floor. Instinctively, he reached for his hip only to encounter air. Since coming home, he hadn't wore his gun in plain sight. Brady saw the motion and knew the reports Allan had given where true. His son had become a gunman. What he didn't see was Nitika hiding her gun in the folds of her skirt.

"How dare you bring that woman into my house," he screamed.

"You're out of jail, I see," Hunter said as calmly as he could.

"I knew they couldn't hold me for long. And you," he fumed pointing a finger at Nitika, "I don't want to see you around here again. You've poisoned this family enough. And you Junior, are going to marry Irena before the day's over."

"Nothing doing," Nitika said from her position on the floor.

"That wasn't a request young lady," he barked. "I will not have you spoil my bloodline."

"It's a bit too late for that," she said, gripping her gun tighter.

"You told me you weren't carrying. Are you telling now that you are?"

"Brady and I are one and you can't do anything about it."

"Get out now," he said stalking closer.

Now fearful, Nitika brought her gun into view, stopping Brady in his tracks. "Like it or not, I am a member of this family."

"You can drop the act Missy. I already know you aren't married to Junior."

"Maybe not yet, but we will be soon," Hunter said coming to stand behind Nitika.

"You marry this woman and you will no longer be a Huntington, Junior."

"I haven't been a Huntington since you sent me to the army. My name is Hunter Tilton now."

"I'll cut you out of the will," Brady declared shaking his finger at the ceiling.

"I don't want your money," Hunter spat. "I never have."

With that said, he grabbed Nitika's hand and left his parent's house. Mary Beth returned from her hurried flight to the kitchen carrying a frying pan. She was willing to fight her own husband if it meant saving her son.

"He may not want your money," she said cooly. "But I will take every penny of it that I can get when I divorce you."

Hansen was driving his hack around town looking for business. With the rich lady and her husband at the Huntington estate, there wasn't anything for him to do. On a whim, he drove toward the stately manor. He saw the young couple come out the gated front entrance as he approached. A frown crossed his face when he didn't like what he saw.

Mr. Huntington was dragging his wife along with him, a scowl on his face. Just past the entrance, the missus dug in her heels and pulled free of his grasp. He turned and began shouting at her, gesturing at the house and pacing around. Worried he was about to hit her, Hansen urged his horse to a trot. By the time he reached them, she had pulled his head down for a kiss.

Nitika could feel Hunter relax in her arms. She had never seen him so angry at anyone before and it was the only way she knew to distract him. He tried to break free, but she refused to release him. When she felt his neck finally unwind, Nitika reluctantly broke the kiss. Hunter pulled her into his arms.

"I'm sorry Sweetheart. I didn't mean to take it out on you. But that man is impossible."

"I know," she said soothingly. "So what's next Mr. Tilton?"

"You folks need a ride," Hansen asked somewhat confused at the sudden change of their moods.

"Yes Hansen, we do," Hunter said looking up at the man. "We need to get to the courthouse and find a judge."

"A judge Sir?"

"Yep, me and Nitika are getting married," he said helping her inside.

"But aren't you already married," the driver asked even more dumbfounded.

"It's a long story," Nitika said through the window.

Hansen shrugged his shoulders as he drove them to the courthouse. He waited outside for them. Mrs. Huntington had called him Mr. Tilton. Word on the street was that Brady Jr. had hired his gun out while living out west. Maybe he was using a different name to keep his family safe. But why would a man as rich as Mr. Huntington feel the need to become a gunman?

Hunter saw Judge Hall coming out of a courtroom and stopped him. Hall was an old friend of his father. He hoped that would keep the judge from asking too many questions. The judge smiled when he saw Hunter coming toward him with a woman in tow. For years, he hoped the young man would find someone and settle down. Being a judge, he knew some about what Brady had been doing since leaving the army. Though he never did anything illegal, the old judge was afraid someone would have a faster draw than Brady some day.

"Brady, it's good to see you. Who's your lady friend?"

"Judge Hall, this is Nitika Brodie," he said wrapping his arm around her waist.

"A pleasure, Ma'am. I'm glad to see that Brady here has found someone. And it's about time, I say. Now, what can I do for you?"

"I'm sure you can guess what it is we want Sir. Nitika and I would like to get married as soon as possible."

"I see," the judge said glancing at Nitika's waist. "I am free for the next hour. That should give you enough time to bring your family down here."

"Actually Sir, I'd rather not wait for them. Father isn't exactly happy about us getting married."

"I'm sorry to hear that. What about your mother? And Miss Brodie's family? I'm sure they'd want to be here."

"Mother is having troubles and I don't want to bother her right now."

"And my family lives in New Mexico," Nitika explained.

"Well I guess if you really want to get married this way, my wife went to get us something to eat. When she comes back, we can have the ceremony then."

While they waited for Mrs. Hall, the judge had them fill out the paperwork. He didn't say anything when Hunter didn't use his real name. His reason behind it was Hunter's own business. The judge only hoped no one would come looking for him using that name.

Hunter looked across the carriage at Nitika. He couldn't believe they actually got married. Now they were on their way back to her hotel room. In the morning, they were going to get on the first train headed back home. Now that his father was no longer dying, he wasn't needed here.

Hunter helped Nitika out of the hack and followed her into the hotel. Matthews was at the desk when they entered the lobby. He saw the bruises still circling Hunter's eyes and whistled softly. His wife did a good number on him when she punched him. The way they were carrying on, all was forgiven about last night and this morning.

A man entered the lobby just behind them. When the couple stopped by the desk to share a kiss, the man closed the distance between them. He grabbed Hunter by the shoulder and spun him around. Matthews saw the man take a swing at Hunter.

Colton couldn't believe his luck. Hunter and Nitika had paused in the lobby long enough for him to catch up with them. He felt that if he could get the drop on Hunter, he had a chance to beat him. Dagon knew he was no match against him if Hunter knew what was happening. He was shocked when Hunter hit the floor with a groan and laid there.

Nitika stepped over Hunter and shoved hard against Colton's shoulders, pushing him away from her husband. "What do you think you're doing?"

"You belong to me and I'm here to prove it." He looked down at Hunter still unmoving on the floor. Colton felt a little disappointed that Hunter wasn't more of a challenge.

"Only a coward fights an injured man," Nitika said bringing his thoughts back to her.

He looked at Hunter again as he rolled onto his back. Colton saw the bruises on his face and knew Hunter wasn't at his best. Nitika shoved against him again, pushing him toward the door.

Chapter 29

"You and I belong together," he insisted as he took a firm stance. He was not going to let a woman push him out the door.

"Maybe in your mind, but Hunter and I are married. And there's nothing you can do about it now."

"I just came from the Pinkerton office. They told me about the fake marriage license you had your friends create. You aren't married to him."

Nitika reached for her reticule and Colton flinched. He knew she carried her gun in there sometimes. She saw him jerk and smirked at him. Colton was a coward in every sense of the word. Showing him the paper she pulled out, Nitika unfolded it and turned it for him to read.

"Devon might have faked one for me, but this one's real."

"No, it can't be," he said unbelieving. "You're mine. You've always been mine. You can't be married to him."

"Sorry to disappoint you, but we are. You're going to have to find another woman to prey on. Irena Braun would be perfect for you. She's just as conniving as you are."

Nitika turned her back on him and went back to the desk. Hunter had managed to stand, though he was leaning against the desk. Wrapping his arm around her shoulders, he followed her up to their room. He sat down on the bed and rubbed his neck.

"Why does everyone think they have to hit me in the face," he moaned. "If this keeps up, I'll never get rid of the black eyes."

"What if I lock you in a room for a couple weeks? Would that get rid of the black eyes," she asked mischievously.

Hunter thought about it for a minute. "That might be kind of fun if you were there with me. Though, we might not get too much sleep."

Nitika answered a knock on their door. Matthews was standing there holding a bowl of ice chips. "I thought you might need these," he said nervously.

"Thank you. That was thoughtful of you," she said accepting the bowl.

"I just wanted to say that I'm sorry for any trouble I might have caused. You know, for sticking my nose where it didn't belong."

"Madeline back home is worse than you. She actually listens at the door. We accept your apology."

Visibly relieved, Matthews bid them farewell and scurried back downstairs. Nitika motioned Hunter to lay down. Taking a small towel, she filled it with the ice and placed it on his eyes. He lifted it when he heard Nitika roaming around the room. She was packing her things, getting ready for the ride back home.

Home sounded good to him right now. He'd had enough of his father's antics and was anxious to get out of here as soon as possible. His next problem was going back to his parent's house to retrieve his things. Hunter felt the bed shift and knew Nitika had crawled on top with him. But before he could do anything, there came another knock on their door.

"Now who can that be," he complained. Setting the ice pack aside, he went to open the door, ready to chew out whoever it was.

Mary Beth was startled when Hunter threw open the door, glaring. She saw the puffiness on his other cheek. "Another fight Dear?"

"Mother," he exclaimed. "What are you doing here?"

"I thought you might want your things if you were heading for home," she said gesturing to the bag at her feet. "And I left your father."

"You what," he said, shocked.

"I left your father. Any man who treats women the way he does, doesn't deserve me."

She walked into the room and sat down on the chair. Hunter reached down for his bag and saw her luggage sitting in the hall. He hauled it into the room and resumed his spot on the bed. Though he wanted to lay down, he needed to know what was going on.

"What you are going to do now?"

"Well, I was hoping Nitika's offer was still good," she said trepidly. "Once the people here find out about the divorce, I won't have any friends left. I thought maybe I could get a fresh start someplace else."

"What offer are you talking about?"

"I told your mother that she could come live with us on the ranch if she had no place to go. There's plenty of room to build a cabin if she didn't mind living in the middle of nowhere."

Nitika looked at him expectantly. Although it was her ranch, it was his mother. If he wasn't comfortable with it, she didn't want to push him into it. But it would be nice to have her around when the time came.

"It's up to you Mother. You're more than welcome to come and live with us. But I've got to warn you, we don't have much of a social life in Sante Fe. You might get bored."

"I'm sure you and Nitika will have plenty of children to keep a grandmother busy."

"Mother," he groaned. "It's too early to be talking about that."

"I see Nitika is wearing your grandmother's ring. So I would say it's probably the right time to be thinking about children." Mary Beth watched crimson rise up Hunter's neck. "Do you mind if I leave my things here until morning? I have a room down the hall for tonight."

"Of course, it'll make it easier to have them taken to the station in the morning," Nitika said as Mary Beth headed for the door.

Hunter left the two women waiting on the bench while he went to check to make sure the train was on time. The sooner they left, the less chance there was of his father finding them. He still couldn't believe his father would go through so much for money. None of that mattered now that Nitika was his and he was going back where he belonged.

"So," Mary Beth said to Nitika, looking over her shoulder at her son, "when are you going to tell him?"

"Tell him what," Nitika asked confused.

"About the baby."

Nitika ducked her head. "I don't know what you're talking about."

"You might be able to hide it from Hunter, but you can't hide it from me. I can see how tight your dress is getting. He's going to suspect it soon enough."

"I was going to tell him last night," Nitika confessed.

"And I spoiled it for you," Mary Beth gasped. "I'm sorry Dear. I shouldn't have imposed like I did. You did just get married last night. You probably wanted time alone and I butted in." She looked back over her shoulder to make sure Hunter wasn't in hearing range. "Would you have told Hunter about the baby if he hadn't married you?"

"I hoped it wouldn't come to that. But I didn't want him to marry me out of obligation."

"My son would have done that," she admitted. "But the way he loves you, I don't think he'd see it that way. Hunter hasn't loved a woman before like he loves you."

Nitika was curled up on Hunter's lap on the front porch a week after coming home, his hand protectively covering her stomach. Since learning about the baby, he had been doting on her until she couldn't take it anymore. She finally had to threaten him with another broken nose to get him to back off.

Dyami was overjoyed about the news of their marriage and his first grandchild. But his joy didn't compare to Nitika's surprise when she arrived home to find him with his new wife and child. Sweet Wolf had somewhat reluctantly left her tribe to come live with him.

She had been afraid of how the people on the ranch would react to her. Thunder Woman had taken the girl in under her wing and was teaching her about life on the ranch.

"I told you the bruises would go away," she said brushing his hair back off his face.

"Yeah well, no one's tried to fight me either. Except you, that is."

Hunter dipped his head to capture her lips in a kiss. So engrossed in each other, they never heard the buggy until it stopped at the hitching post. Sweet Wolf had heard someone enter the yard and came to see who it was. She stood just behind the screen door, curious about the white couple.

"That is no way for a young lady to act," Odelia huffed.

Nitika broke off the kiss suddenly and stared at her mother. "Mother, what are you doing here?"

"Can't I come see my own daughter when I want to," she said accusingly.

"Of course. I didn't mean it the way it sounded. Hello Charles."

"Miss Nitika. It's good to see you again."

"Who is this man you're wrapped around," Odelia asked icily.

"My husband, Hunter Tilton."

"You couldn't see fit to invite your own mother to the wedding?"

"We didn't have a regular wedding. It was kind of a hurried ceremony."

Odelia saw where Hunter's hand was laying. "I can see why. Just what would your father think of how you've turned out?"

"I'm quite pleased with her, Odelia," Dyami said coming around the corner of the house.

Chapter 30

Odelia stared open-mouthed at the man who stood before her. Realization hit her and she sank back against the seat of her buggy. Charles wrapped his arm around her, afraid she was going to faint. With shaky hands, she brushed him off and climbed down. Dyami was alive. As she got closer to him, she saw the scars on his face and stopped dead in her tracks.

Dyami watched her compose herself before she spoke. "What happened to your face?"

"The explosion, remember. I was nearly killed in it."

"Why did you not tell me you were still alive," she asked turning away from him.

"Would you have let me in the house if I had," he asked her coming up to her.

"I don't know," she stammered stepping away from him.

Seeing that he was making her nervous, Dyami walked past her and up onto the porch. Sweet Wolf came out carrying Fawn. Odelia looked to see who came out of the house. She saw the Indian woman hand Dyami the baby girl.

"Who is she," she asked Nitika.

"Sakari Tala," Sweet Wolf said. "I am Dyami's wife. This is our daughter Awentia."

"I see it didn't take you long to find another wife. She the one you've been living with since you left me?"

"Odelia, it took me almost a year to fully heal from my injuries. It was Sweet Wolf's tribe that found me and treated my injuries. I didn't leave you. You had me declared dead and our marriage annulled. What was I supposed to do then?"

"How do you know all that," she asked accusingly.

"I had a lawyer check into it for me. I wanted to know for sure if we were still married or not."

"Why? So you could marry her," Odelia said flicking her fingers as Sweet Wolf.

"No. Nitika told me you had found someone. I wanted to make sure there weren't complications for you."

"What gave you the right to tell him Angel?"

"He's my father. He deserved to know."

Feeling out of place, Hunter gently moved Nitika to the settee by herself. "I've got work to do. I'll be back in time for supper."

Hunter sidestepped Odelia as he headed for the barn. He understood now why Nitika was reluctant to get married. How Dyami could love a such cold hearted woman like that, he didn't know. The woman couldn't bear to look him in the face once she saw the scars. If she felt any love at all for him, what he looked like wouldn't matter.

Odelia watched Hunter's retreating back. Nitika had married below her class. That's what falling in love did to a woman. It made her blind to the fact that her husband was living off her money alone, unlike her relationship with Charles. He had plenty of money for both of them. She only hoped that this man wouldn't bleed her daughter dry. The last thing she wanted was to have Nitika coming home to live with her again.

"Aren't you going to invite us in," Odelia asked haughtily.

"Must I," Nitika mumbled under her breath. Dyami gave her a reprimanding look. "Of course," she said to her mother, "how could I have been so inhospitable?"

Mary Beth came down the stairs as everyone came in the front door. She was covered head to toe in a layer of dust. Dressed in an old outfit , her hair covered by a kerchief, she had been digging out baby things from the attic. Now conscious of her appearance, she tried futilely to brush away the grime.

"Forgive me for the way I look. I didn't know we had company."

"Do you let all the hired help walk around like this," Odelia asked Nitika.

"Mother, I'd like you to meet my mother in law, Mary Beth Huntington. Mary Beth this is my mother, Odelia. Is it still Brodie, or did you change it?"

"How dare you ask me a question like that in front of-," Odelia paused. "Did you say this is your mother in law?"

"That's right. Her name is Mary Beth Huntington. As in Huntington Freighting Company."

"But you just said your husband's name is Tilton. How can that be?"

"Brady changed his name to Hunter Tilton," Mary Beth explained. "And I respect his wishes to do so. But yes, he is my son."

"Mrs. Huntington, I do hope you forgive my rude comments. It has been a very long trip and I am quite tired. I simply don't know what I am saying."

"I take no offense. I am a sight right now. I was up in the attic looking for the baby furniture Nitika said is up there. In her condition, I didn't feel it was right for her to be crawling around up there."

"Yes, that is something we need to talk about, young lady," Odelia said turning to Nitika. "Among other things."

"Leave her alone Odelia," Dyami said coming up behind Nitika. "You made it clear that you weren't raising Nitika when she was a child. If she isn't the lady you want her to be, it's your own fault."

Odelia turned to Nitika. "Is there some place I can lay down? I'm really tired."

"Do you remember where the guest room is?"

"Of course," Odelia said frostily. "Is that the only room available?"

Dyami's hand on her shoulder was the only thing that kept Nitika from saying what was really on her tongue. Her mother was just as hard now as she ever was. Odelia had tried to turn Nitika into a younger version of herself once she realized that Nitika was sixteen. By then, Dyami had raised her to be herself taking away Odelia's chance to make her a lady.

"Until the men finish building the other houses, yes the only bedroom open is the guest room."

"Houses? I'm surprised anyone would want to live out here in this desolate place."

"One house is for me and the other one is for Mary Beth," Dyami explained. "We don't want to impose too long on Nitika and Hunter."

"Will Mr. Huntington be joining you?"

"No. Brady and I are no longer together. We had a difference of opinion and I left him."

Odelia only smiled contritely. "Well, if you'll excuse me."

Nitika's patience wore out once she heard the door close behind her mother. "What gives her the right to berate me in my own home? She didn't want anything to do with me growing up. Why does she want in now?"

"I don't know Darling. She's not the same person I married. I know that for sure. Maybe it's this new man Charles. Although he seems to be henpecked already. He's barely spoke since they got here."

"Mother hasn't changed Father. I think maybe you have. As for Charles, he knows how to handle her without her knowing. I've seen him to get her to do things I thought she'd never do. She never did tell me why she's here."

"Maybe she's here to announce a marriage."

"Maybe Mother thought she was coming to plan mine. That could explain her foul mood."

"She always defies me," Odelia fumed once they reached the guest room. "She is too headstrong for her own good sometimes. The nerve of her to get married without me there."

"Like mother like daughter," Charles said quietly.

Odelia turned on him. "It isn't the same."

About the Author

This is the second book in the Pink Angel series. Hunter's Past is the story behind how Nitika and Hunter ended up meeting and the secrets that Hunter didn't want her to know. This author decided to dabble with the idea of a stalker and the length he would go to get the woman he wanted. Whether that was accomplished or not is up to the reader.